FOR INFORMATION OR PERMISSIONS,
PLEASE CONTACT: CONNECT@PHOENYXJROSE.COM
COVER AND INTERIOR DESIGN BY: TIRADO DESIGNS
PUBLISHED BY: JMARIE & CO. PUBLISHING
ISBN: 978-1-968115-02-9
PRINTED IN UNITED STATES OF AMERICA

# THINGS WE NEVER SAID

## THE SILAS HAWTHORNE LETTERS

# PHOENYX J. ROSE

# DEAR MARE,
## THE LETTERS I NEVER SENT

SILAS MONROE HAWTHORNE

APRIL 5, 2004

DEAR MARE,

YOU PUT THE WATCH ON MY WRIST, AND I LET YOU.
I DIDN'T STOP YOU. I DIDN'T ASK WHAT IT MEANT.
I DIDN'T SAY YOUR NAME THE WAY I WANTED TO—LIKE A PRAYER WITH BLOOD IN IT.
YOU DIDN'T CRY. YOU DIDN'T RAGE. YOU BUTTONED YOUR SHIRT, KISSED MY JAW, AND SAID, "DID YOU EVER REALLY LOVE ME."
AND THEN YOU WALKED OUT THE FRONT DOOR LIKE IT WASN'T GOING TO KILL ME.
YOU LEFT NOTHING BEHIND EXCEPT YOUR WARMTH IN MY SHEETS AND THE WEIGHT OF THAT WATCH ON MY SKIN.
IT'S HEAVY, MARE. I SWEAR TO GOD, IT'S SO FUCKING HEAVY.
I WON'T TAKEN IT OFF.
NOT BECAUSE I WANT TO KEEP IT—
BECAUSE I DON'T KNOW WHAT HAPPENS IF I DO.
YOU GAVE ME TWO YEARS.
TWO YEARS OF YOU CHOOSING ME.
TWO YEARS OF ME NOT BEING BRAVE ENOUGH TO CHOOSE YOU BACK.
I WANTED TO.
EVERY DAMN DAY, I WANTED TO.
BUT I NEVER TOLD YOU I LOVED YOU. I NEVER HELD YOU IN DAYLIGHT. I NEVER MADE YOU REAL.

AND TONIGHT?
 YOU WERE THE REALEST THING IN
MY HOUSE. NOW YOU'RE GONE.
AND I'M WEARING TIME LIKE A
NOOSE.
IF I COULD GO BACK, I'D TAKE
YOUR HAND AND NEVER LET GO.
IF I COULD GO FORWARD, I'D FIND
A VERSION OF ME THAT NEVER MADE
YOU DOUBT WHAT YOU MEANT.
BUT ALL I HAVE IS NOW.
 AND THIS LETTER.
 AND THE ECHO OF YOUR FINGERS
ON MY WRIST.
HAPPY BIRTHDAY, MARE.
I'M SORRY I RUINED THIS.
 I'M SORRY I RUINED YOU.
— S

DEAR ~~MARIS~~ MARE, MY MARE

I DIDN'T SLEEP.
I LAID IN OUR BED—MINE AND SARAH'S—
AND FELT LIKE I WAS CHEATING ON YOU
WITH THE MEMORY OF WHO I USED TO BE.
THE SHEETS STILL SMELLED LIKE YOU. I
HAVEN'T CHANGED THEM.  I COULDN'T.
NOT YET.
YOUR NAME IS IN MY THROAT LIKE SMOKE,
AND EVERY TIME I SWALLOW IT BACK, I
FEEL SOMETHING INSIDE ME BURN.
SARAH COMES HOME TODAY.
I DON'T KNOW HOW TO LOOK AT HER AND
NOT FLINCH.
 I DON'T KNOW HOW TO PRETEND THAT I'M
NOT BROKEN OPEN FROM THE INSIDE OUT.
SHE'S GOING TO ASK IF I'M OKAY. SHE
ALWAYS DOES.
 SHE WON'T ASK WHY I DIDN'T CALL LAST
NIGHT, BECAUSE I'VE BUILT MY SILENCES
WELL.
 SHE'LL KISS MY CHEEK AND UNPACK HER
SUITCASE AND I'LL NOD AND LIE AND EAT
AND LIE AND BREATHE AND LIE.
YOU MADE ME REAL, MARE.
 EVEN WHEN I DIDN'T DESERVE IT.

AND NOW I'M A MAN AGAIN WITH A
SHADOW WHERE HIS HEART USED TO BE.
THE WATCH IS STILL ON MY WRIST.
 I KEEP LOOKING AT IT LIKE YOU MIGHT
WALK BACK IN THE DOOR AND TAKE IT
BACK.
 LIKE YOU MIGHT KISS ME ONCE MORE
BEFORE THE MASK GOES ON FOR GOOD.
BUT YOU WON'T. YOU SHOULDN'T.
YOU GAVE ME TIME, AND I WASTED IT.
 NOW I'M WEARING IT LIKE
PUNISHMENT.
IF I MAKE IT THROUGH TODAY WITHOUT
FALLING APART, IT'LL BE A MIRACLE.
BUT MAYBE I DESERVE THE
PERFORMANCE.
 MAYBE THAT'S THE PENANCE FOR
LOVING YOU IN SECRET AND LOSING
YOU IN SILENCE.
I MISS YOU ALREADY.
 AND I HATE MYSELF FOR NOT STOPPING
YOU.
—S

DEAR MARE,
I'VE BEEN SLEEPING ON THE COUCH.
I TOLD SARAH IT'S BECAUSE MY BACK
WAS HURTING. THAT WAS A LIE. THE
REAL REASON IS THAT I WOKE UP
SCREAMING YOUR NAME THREE NIGHTS
AGO, AND SHE HEARD ME.
SHE DIDN'T CRY.  DIDN'T THROW
ANYTHING.
SHE JUST STOOD THERE IN THE DARK
WITH HER ARMS CROSSED AND ASKED,
"ARE YOU HAVING AN AFFAIR?"
I TOLD HER THE TRUTH—NOT ANYMORE.
PHYSICALLY, IT'S OVER. BUT YOU AND
I BOTH KNOW HOW FUCKING FAR THAT
IS FROM <u>DONE</u>.
WHAT I DIDN'T TELL HER IS THAT I
STILL TASTE YOUR NAME EVERY TIME I
OPEN MY MOUTH.
THAT I'M GOING THROUGH WITHDRAWAL
LIKE YOU WERE A DRUG AND I'M
WHITE-KNUCKLING SOBRIETY ONE
BREATH AT A TIME.

SHE DOESN'T KNOW I KEEP LOOKING AT
THE FRONT DOOR LIKE YOU MIGHT WALK
THROUGH IT.
THAT I KEEP CHECKING THE MIRROR TO
SEE IF I LOOK LIKE A MAN YOU'D
STILL WANT.
  THAT I'VE REWRITTEN THIS LETTER
FOUR TIMES TONIGHT AND STILL CAN'T
FIND A WAY TO STOP MISSING YOU.
YOU SAID I NEVER CHOSE YOU.
  YOU WERE RIGHT.
AND NOW THE SILENCE YOU LEFT BEHIND
IS LOUDER THAN ANYTHING I'VE EVER
HEARD.
I'VE BEEN THINKING ABOUT HOW I SAID
YOUR NAME IN MY SLEEP. NOT HERS.
YOURS.
AND IF THAT'S NOT A CONFESSION, I
DON'T KNOW WHAT IS.
THE SHIRT I'M WEARING STILL SMELLS
LIKE THE DETERGENT YOU USED WHEN I
STAYED THE NIGHT AT YOUR PLACE. THE
NIGHT YOU READ YOUR WRITING TO ME
UNTIL I FELL ASLEEP.
I DON'T THINK I'LL EVER SLEEP
AGAIN.
—S

APRIL 25, 2004

I CARVED THIS INTO A WOODEN
BOX TODAY. EVERYTHING YOU
LEFT IS IN IT NOW. I DREW IT
OVER AND OVER AGAIN TO GET
IT JUST RIGHT. JUST LIKE THE
ONE I'VE KISSED ON YOUR HIP
A THOUSAND TIMES. I STILL
REMEMBER THE SOUND YOU
MADE WHEN I KISSED IT THE
FIRST TIME, WHEN IT WAS
STILL TENDER.

I THINK YOU'D LOVE IT. YOU
ALWAYS WANTED ME TO BUILD
YOU SOMETHING.

DEAR MARE                          JUNE 28, 2004

I SAID YOUR NAME WHEN I CAME LAST
NIGHT. I WASN'T EVEN THINKING ABOUT
YOU—NOT CONSCIOUSLY.
 BUT MY BODY REMEMBERED. MY MOUTH
REMEMBERED. EVERYTHING IN ME
REMEMBERED YOU.
SARAH AND I HAD BEEN TRYING. TRYING TO
PRETEND WE WEREN'T BROKEN. TRYING
TO FORGET HOW I USED TO SLEEP ON THE
COUCH AND CRY INTO MY HANDS.
SHE ASKED IF WE COULD BE PHYSICAL
AGAIN. I SAID YES, BECAUSE I THOUGHT
MAYBE THAT WOULD HELP.
WE USED TO HAVE THIS... ROUTINE. QUIET.
SAFE. MOSTLY MISSIONARY. SHE'D CLOSE
HER EYES, AND I'D PRETEND I DIDN'T
NOTICE. BUT THIS TIME?
THIS TIME I TOUCHED HER LIKE I TOUCH
YOU. I GRABBED HER. I FLIPPED HER.
 I PUSHED HER FACE INTO THE PILLOW AND
GROWLED AGAINST HER SKIN.
 AND SHE DIDN'T STOP ME. SHE MOANED
LIKE SHE DIDN'T KNOW SHE HAD THAT
SOUND IN HER.

BUT I WASN'T WITH HER. I WAS WITH
YOU. AND WHEN I CAME, IT WASN'T HER
NAME THAT LEFT MY MOUTH.
IT WAS YOURS. MARE. LOUD. CRACKED.
RAW.
THE SECOND IT SLIPPED OUT, EVERYTHING
FROZE. SHE PULLED AWAY LIKE I'D HIT
HER.
SHE JUST SAT ON THE EDGE OF THE BED,
BREATHING HARD, STARING AT THE FLOOR.
THEN SHE PACKED HER BAG AND LEFT.
THAT WAS SIX HOURS AGO. THE BEDROOM
STILL SMELLS LIKE HER. BUT THE MIRROR
SMELLS LIKE YOU.
I DON'T KNOW WHAT I'M DOING. I DON'T
KNOW WHO I AM ANYMORE. BUT I KNOW
WHO I WAS WITH YOU.
AND I KNOW WHAT I LOST. I HAVEN'T TAKEN
THE WATCH OFF. NOT ONCE.
IT'S THE ONLY PART OF ME THAT FEELS
HONEST ANYMORE.
—S

I WASN'T GOING TO WRITE YOU. I TOLD
MYSELF I WAS DONE BLEEDING ON PAGES
YOU'LL NEVER READ.
 I SWORE I WOULDN'T CHASE GHOSTS
ANYMORE. BUT THEN I SAW YOU TODAY. AT
LEAST—I THOUGHT I DID.
SHE WAS CROSSING THE STREET. SAME
GOLDEN-BROWN SKIN. SAME CURLS, WILD
AND SOFT LIKE THE WAY YOUR HAIR USED TO
FALL WHEN YOU WEREN'T TRYING TO BE
ANYTHING FOR ANYONE.
SHE LAUGHED. TIPPED HER HEAD THE SAME
WAY YOU DO WHEN YOU'RE FLIRTING WITH
YOUR OWN THOUGHTS. I SWEAR TO GOD,
MARE, MY HEART STOPPED.
I CROSSED TWO LANES OF TRAFFIC WITHOUT
LOOKING. RAN LIKE I WAS TRYING TO CATCH
MY LIFE BEFORE IT LEFT AGAIN. I CALLED
YOUR NAME. **"MARE!"** LOUD. DESPERATE.
FUCKING EMBARRASSING.
SHE TURNED AROUND. OF COURSE IT WASN'T
YOU. OF COURSE. SHE LOOKED AT ME LIKE I
WAS INSANE.
 I PROBABLY WAS.

I MUMBLED SOMETHING. APOLOGIZED.
TRIED TO SMILE LIKE IT DIDN'T
SHATTER ME.
 BUT IT DID. IT FUCKING BROKE ME,
MARE.
BECAUSE FOR HALF A SECOND, I FELT
THAT PULSE AGAIN. THE ONE I ONLY
EVER FELT WHEN YOU WERE CLOSE
ENOUGH TO RUIN ME. AND THEN IT
TURNED OUT TO BE SMOKE.  I REACHED
FOR FIRE, AND THE WORLD HANDED ME
SMOKE.
I WALKED BACK TO MY CAR IN SILENCE.
 SAT THERE FOR I DON'T KNOW HOW
LONG WITH MY HANDS IN MY LAP,
WONDERING IF I'LL EVER STOP
REACHING FOR YOUR GHOST.
I TRIED NOT TO WRITE. I FAILED.
—S

# FUCK

SEPTEMBER 18, 2004

DEAR **MARE**,

I WENT OUT TONIGHT. BACHELOR PARTY. MY BROTHER. STRIP CLUB. THE WHOLE DAMN CLICHÉ.

I TOLD MYSELF I'D BE PRESENT. THAT I'D DRINK. LAUGH. BE NORMAL AGAIN. TURNS OUT, NORMAL IS JUST A COSTUME I DON'T FIT INTO ANYMORE.

THEY BROUGHT OUT THIS WOMAN— TALL. CURVY. GOLDEN SKIN. CURLS PULLED INTO A MESSY UPDO.

SHE LOOKED ENOUGH LIKE YOU THAT MY BREATH CAUGHT.

SHE SAT ON MY LAP. STRADDLED ME LIKE MUSCLE MEMORY. RAN HER FINGERS THROUGH MY HAIR AND ASKED IF I WANTED A PRIVATE DANCE.

I LOOKED HER RIGHT IN THE EYE AND SAID,

**"CAN I CALL YOU MARE?"**

SHE SAID, **"SURE, BABY."** YOUR VOICE WASN'T THERE. THE EDGE OF SARCASM, THE SOFT SMOKE IN YOUR VOWELS, THE WAY YOU SAY MY NAME LIKE IT'S A DARE— **NONE OF IT WAS THERE.** BUT I DIDN'T STOP HER. I LET HER ROCK HER HIPS AGAINST ME LIKE SHE KNEW ME.

I LET HER MOUTH GRAZE MY EAR. I ~~LET HER SAY YOUR NAME LIKE SHE'D~~ EARNED IT.
AND IT WORKED. FOR A SECOND. JUST ENOUGH TO MAKE ME HARD AGAIN.
JUST ENOUGH TO FEEL YOU IN MY BLOODSTREAM LIKE A FIX. NOT THE REAL THING.
BUT CLOSE ENOUGH TO MAKE IT THROUGH THE NIGHT WITHOUT FALLING APART.
WHEN SHE LEFT, I FELT SICK. I WENT TO THE BATHROOM, SPLASHED COLD WATER ON MY FACE, LOOKED IN THE MIRROR— AND I DIDN'T SEE MYSELF. I SAW A MAN WHO USED TO BE LOVED BY YOU.
I DON'T KNOW WHAT I HATE MORE. THAT I USED HER. OR THAT I COULDN'T EVEN ENJOY IT WITHOUT IMAGINING YOU. MAYBE IT'S BOTH. MAYBE THAT'S ALL I HAVE LEFT NOW.
SUBSTITUTES.
—S

NOV 2, 2004

MARE,

I SIGNED THE PAPERS TODAY. NO CEREMONY. NO SCREAMING. NO THROWN PLATES OR DRAMATIC EXITS. JUST A PEN, A NOTARY, AND A SILENCE THAT DIDN'T FEEL NEARLY AS SATISFYING AS I THOUGHT IT WOULD.
IT SHOULD HAVE MEANT SOMETHING. IT SHOULD'VE FELT LIKE FREEDOM.
INSTEAD, ALL I COULD THINK ABOUT WAS THE NIGHT YOU LEFT. YOU IN THAT DAMN HOODIE, STANDING IN THE DOORWAY WITH YOUR HANDS IN YOUR POCKETS LIKE IF YOU DIDN'T MOVE TOO MUCH, IT WOULDN'T HURT.
YOU DIDN'T CRY. YOU DIDN'T ASK ME TO CHASE YOU.
I STILL DON'T KNOW IF THAT MADE IT EASIER OR WORSE.
SHE ASKED ME IF THERE WAS SOMEONE ELSE.
I TOLD HER THE TRUTH.
"THERE WAS." YOU WERE.
SHE DIDN'T ASK YOUR NAME. I THINK SHE ALREADY KNEW. OR MAYBE SHE DIDN'T CARE.
WE HADN'T BEEN IN LOVE FOR YEARS.

SHE DIDN'T LEAVE CLAW MARKS.
YOU DID. THE TRUTH IS, I WAS
ALREADY DIVORCED THE NIGHT YOU
SHOWED UP IN THAT BAR AND
RUINED ME WITH YOUR LAUGHTER
AND HORRIBLE KARAOKE RENDITION
OF MUSTANG SALLY. TODAY JUST
MADE IT LEGAL.
AND NOW I'M SITTING HERE IN
THIS EMPTY APARTMENT THAT
ECHOES WHEN I TALK TOO LOUD,
WRITING TO A WOMAN WHO WILL
NEVER READ THESE WORDS.
BUT I HAVE TO WRITE THEM.
BECAUSE IF I DON'T, THEY'LL
TURN INTO SOMETHING ELSE.
SOMETHING DARKER.
SOMETHING I WON'T SURVIVE.
I MISS YOU EVERY SECOND, MARE.
AND I HATE THAT MISSING YOU IS
THE CLOSEST I CAN GET TO
TOUCHING YOU.
ALWAYS,
S

DEC 25, 2004

MARE,


IT'S CHRISTMAS. MY BROTHER GAVE ME
A BOTTLE OF WHISKEY.  MY MOM MADE
THAT CASSEROLE I HATE BUT ALWAYS
PRETEND TO EAT.
 I WORE THE SWEATER SARAH'S SISTER
GAVE ME LAST YEAR.  NO ONE SAID HER
NAME. NOT ONCE.
I SMILED ALL DAY.  I OPENED
PRESENTS. I LAUGHED AT THE RIGHT
TIMES. I ASKED ABOUT JOBS, BABIES,
DOGS, PROMOTIONS.
AND THE WHOLE TIME, I KEPT HEARING
YOUR VOICE IN MY HEAD, WHISPERING,
**"YOU HATE SMALL TALK. YOU'RE
FIDGETING. GO OUTSIDE."**
I DID. I WENT OUTSIDE AFTER DINNER.
 LIT A CIGARETTE. I DON'T SMOKE
ANYMORE, NOT SINCE THE DAY YOU
LEFT, BUT TONIGHT FELT LIKE AN
EXCEPTION.
THE STARS LOOKED LIKE THE ONES WE
USED TO MAKE UP STORIES ABOUT.  YOU
REMEMBER? THAT SUMMER NIGHT IN
ASHEVILLE ON THE ROOFTOP. YOU MADE
ME NAME EVERY ONE LIKE THEY WERE
CHARACTERS IN A BOOK YOU HADN'T
WRITTEN YET.

YOU CALLED THE BRIGHT ONE
"BELONGING."
I NEVER FORGOT THAT. AND I
HAVEN'T BELONGED ANYWHERE
SINCE YOU LEFT. I THOUGHT
ABOUT TEXTING YOU TODAY. JUST
"MERRY CHRISTMAS."
JUST TO SEE IF THE NUMBER
STILL WORKS.
JUST TO HEAR YOUR SILENCE ON
THE OTHER END.
BUT I DIDN'T. YOU DON'T
DESERVE TO BE HAUNTED BY MY
NOSTALGIA. SO I'M WRITING YOU
THIS LETTER INSTEAD.
NOT BECAUSE I THINK YOU'LL
READ IT.
BUT BECAUSE IT'S CHRISTMAS,
AND ALL I WANTED TO SAY
WAS I STILL MISS YOU. MORE
THAN WHISKEY. MORE THAN
WARMTH. YOU WERE MY FIRE,
MARE. AND NOW IT'S FUCKING
COLD.
— S

MARCH 3, 2005

MARE,

I FINALLY **SAW YOU** TODAY, MARE. YOU WERE SITTING OUTSIDE THAT LITTLE BISTRO YOU ALWAYS LIKED ON GRANT. LAUGHING. **PREGNANT**. HOLDING YOUR BELLY LIKE IT HELD EVERYTHING YOU EVER WANTED.

**GOD. I CAN'T BELIEVE YOU'RE PREGNANT.**

YOU WERE BEAUTIFUL. GLOWING. I'M SURE YOU DIDN'T NOTICE ME. YOU WERE WITH THREE WOMEN AND A GUY.

ONE WOMAN REACHED ACROSS THE TABLE AND TOUCHED YOUR HAND—SAID SOMETHING THAT MADE YOU SMILE SO WIDE, I SWEAR IT PUNCHED THE AIR OUT OF MY LUNGS. YOU WERE WEARING AN ENGAGEMENT RING.

I STOOD ACROSS THE STREET FOR TEN MINUTES. MAYBE LONGER. FROZEN. WATCHING YOU LIVE A LIFE THAT CLEARLY DIDN'T NEED ME IN IT.

YOU LOOKED SO FUCKING HAPPY.

AND I HATED HOW MUCH I LOVED SEEING YOU LIKE THAT.

I WALKED AWAY BEFORE YOU COULD
SEE ME.
  NOT BECAUSE I WAS AFRAID.
  BECAUSE I DIDN'T WANT TO PUT
GRIEF ON YOUR PLATE WHILE YOU
WERE FEEDING JOY TO EVERYONE
AROUND YOU.
  YOU LOOKED PEACEFUL.
  LIKE YOU HAD FOUND A WORLD
THAT DIDN'T CRACK WHEN YOU
TOUCHED IT.
  AND I REALIZED...
  MAYBE I WAS THE ONE WHO BROKE
EVERYTHING.
  MAYBE LOVING YOU WITH THAT KIND
OF FERAL, CONSUMING HUNGER
DIDN'T LEAVE YOU SPACE TO
BREATHE.

THE GUY HOLDING YOUR HAND LOOKED
STEADY.
THE KIND OF MAN WHO DOESN'T RUN WILD
THROUGH YOUR SOUL BUT BUILDS WALLS AND
ROOFS AND CLOSETS WITH MATCHING
HANGERS.
HE LOOKED LIKE COMFORT.
AND YOU—
YOU LOOKED LIKE YOU FINALLY EXHALED.
I WENT HOME AND WROTE THIS LETTER
INSTEAD OF SMASHING THE FUCK OUT OF
SOMETHING. PROGRESS, I GUESS.
BUT MY HANDS ARE SHAKING.
AND I CAN STILL SEE YOUR SMILE EVERY
TIME I CLOSE MY EYES.
I WANT TO FUCKING HATE HIM.
I WANT TO BELIEVE HE STOLE YOU.
BUT THE TRUTH IS, MARE—
YOU WERE NEVER MINE TO KEEP.
JUST MINE TO LOVE.
AND I DID.
GOD, I DID. AND I HATE MYSELF FOR NEVER
SAYING THE WORDS.
I LOVE YOU, MARE.
ALWAYS,
S

JULY 16, 2007

DEAR MARE

IT'S BEEN TWO YEARS. FUCK. TWO YEARS.
I HAVEN'T WRITTEN. NOT BECAUSE I DIDN'T
WANT TO— BECAUSE I DIDN'T THINK I
DESERVED TO.
BUT TODAY I WALKED ACROSS A STAGE AND
TOOK A PIECE OF PAPER THAT SAYS I FINISHED
SOMETHING.
THAT I FOLLOWED THROUGH. THAT I BECAME
THE MAN I ALWAYS SWORE I'D GROW INTO
SOMEDAY.
I HAVE A MASTER'S NOW. COMMUNICATIONS.
IRONIC, RIGHT? THE MAN WHO NEVER SAID
THE RIGHT WORDS FINALLY HAS A DEGREE IN
THEM.
AND YOU WERE THE FIRST PERSON I WANTED
TO TELL. NOT MY MOTHER. NOT MY
BROTHER.
NOT THE FRIENDS I STILL DON'T KNOW HOW
TO BE HONEST WITH. YOU.
BECAUSE IF YOU WERE HERE—IF YOU WERE
REAL AND REACHABLE AND STILL MINE—I
THINK YOU'D SMILE.
I THINK YOU'D CALL ME PROFESSOR JUST TO
TEASE. I THINK YOU'D SAY "IT'S ABOUT
DAMN TIME."
AND I THINK I'D FINALLY SAY, "I DID IT FOR
ME... BUT I STARTED BECAUSE OF YOU."

YOU SAID I NEVER FINISHED ANYTHING. THAT I LIVED IN POTENTIAL LIKE IT WAS ENOUGH. THAT I WANTED GREATNESS BUT WOULDN'T BLEED FOR IT. SO I BLED. QUIETLY. EVERY DEADLINE. EVERY DRAFT. EVERY NIGHT I SAT IN MY APARTMENT WITH YOUR NAME STILL ECHOING IN MY RIBCAGE AND PUSHED THROUGH THE SILENCE.
YOU WERE THE VOICE THAT GOT ME HERE. NOT THE PRETTY ONE. NOT THE SOFT ONE. THE ONE THAT SAID "DO BETTER." SO I DID.
I DON'T KNOW WHERE YOU ARE. I DON'T KNOW IF YOU'D EVER WANT TO KNOW THIS. BUT I WANTED TO SAY IT ANYWAY. I FINISHED. AND PART OF ME DID IT BECAUSE YOU LEFT.
—S

JULY 18, 2007

I HAD SEX TONIGHT. FOR THE FIRST TIME IN YEARS.

I'M WRITING IT LIKE THAT—FLAT, PLAIN, WITHOUT EMBELLISHMENT—BECAUSE I CAN'T PRETEND IT WAS ANYTHING MORE THAN WHAT IT WAS. IT WASN'T LOVE.

IT WASN'T CONNECTION. IT WASN'T **YOU**.

HER NAME WAS CELINE, I THINK. SHE HAD KIND EYES AND CALLED ME HANDSOME WHEN I LOOKED LIKE SHIT. SHE KISSED LIKE SHE'D BEEN WAITING TO BE NOTICED, AND I THINK I TOUCHED HER LIKE I'D FORGOTTEN HOW.

I TRIED. GOD, I TRIED TO STAY PRESENT. TO STAY INSIDE THAT MOMENT, NOT OUR MOMENTS.

BUT THEN HER NAILS BRUSHED THE BACK OF MY NECK AND I FLINCHED LIKE SHE'D BURNED ME. BECAUSE THAT'S WHERE YOU USED TO REST YOUR FINGERS, REMEMBER? LIGHT. COMMANDING. LIKE A QUESTION MARK CURLED BEHIND MY SPINE.

SHE DIDN'T NOTICE. OR MAYBE SHE DID AND DIDN'T CARE. I DIDN'T COME. I TOLD HER I WAS TIRED. SHE SMILED LIKE SHE UNDERSTOOD AND ASKED IF I WANTED

TO STAY. I DIDN'T WANT TO, BUT I DID ANYWAY.

I LAID THERE WITH MY ARM AROUND A STRANGER AND THOUGHT ABOUT THE WAY YOUR BREATH USED TO HITCH WHEN I KISSED THE INSIDE OF YOUR KNEE. HOW YOUR VOICE DROPPED WHEN YOU SAID MY NAME IN THE DARK. I THOUGHT ABOUT THE MORNING AFTER THE FIRST TIME I HAD YOU—WHEN YOU ROLLED OVER, PULLED MY FACE TO YOUR CHEST, AND SAID, "SILAS, WHAT THE FUCK DID YOU DO TO ME?"

I DIDN'T HAVE THE COURAGE TO SAY IT THEN, BUT THE TRUTH WAS: YOU MADE ME SOMEONE WORTH WANTING. AND NOW? NOW I FEEL LIKE I'M JUST BORROWING THE IDEA OF INTIMACY FROM PEOPLE WHO DON'T KNOW WHAT IT ACTUALLY MEANS.

I DON'T KNOW WHY I'M WRITING THIS.

MAYBE BECAUSE IT'S THE ONLY WAY I KNOW HOW TO BE HONEST ANYMORE.

EVEN IF YOU NEVER READ IT.

EVEN IF I NEVER SEND IT.

EVEN IF YOU NEVER LOVED ME THE WAY I LOVED YOU.

THIS WAS MY PENANCE.

AND STILL...

I'D DO IT ALL AGAIN.

YOURS IN THE QUIET,

SILAS

AUG 30 2007

DEAR MARE,
I GOT THE JOB. EDITOR.
NOT ASSISTANT. NOT FREELANCE
CONTRIBUTOR.
EDITOR AT VERVE.
THEY DIDN'T HAND ME THE TITLE THAT
RUNS THE MASTHEAD—NOT YET.
BUT THEY GAVE ME THE PAGES. THE VOICE.
THE ROOM.
AND FOR THE FIRST TIME, I DIDN'T FEEL
LIKE AN IMPOSTER.
I FELT LIKE A MAN BECOMING THE
HEADLINE.
YOU WERE THE FIRST PERSON I WANTED TO
TELL.
NOT TO IMPRESS YOU. NOT TO WIN YOU
BACK.
BECAUSE I KNOW I LOST THAT CHANCE WHEN
I LET YOU WALK AWAY WEARING MY
SILENCE LIKE A FUNERAL DRESS.
BUT STILL— YOU'RE THE VOICE THAT LIVES
BETWEEN THE LINES. I WALKED INTO THAT
OFFICE TODAY WEARING A TIE YOU
WOULD'VE HATED.
TOO CORPORATE. TOO SAFE.
I WORE IT ANYWAY, BECAUSE BECOMING
THE MAN YOU ONCE BELIEVED I COULD BE
MEANT LEARNING HOW TO BLEND IN JUST
LONG ENOUGH TO BREAK OUT.

I SAID THE RIGHT THINGS. QUOTED BALDWIN.
CRACKED A JOKE ABOUT EDITORIAL EGO THAT
MADE THE ROOM LAUGH. I SIGNED THE OFFER
LETTER WITH A PEN THEY HANDED ME—
BUT I THOUGHT ABOUT THE ONE YOU ONCE
GAVE ME FOR MY BIRTHDAY.
THE ONE I NEVER USED. THE ONE THAT
ALWAYS FELT TOO HONEST.
AFTER THE MEETING, I SAT IN MY CAR,
CLOSED MY EYES, AND WHISPERED YOUR
NAME.
MARE.

IT CAME OUT LIKE REVERENCE. LIKE RITUAL.
LIKE PUNCTUATION AT THE END OF A
SENTENCE I'VE BEEN REWRITING FOR THREE
YEARS.
YOU USED TO READ VERVE IN BED WITH
YOUR FOOT TUCKED UNDER MY THIGH,
ROLLING YOUR EYES AT THE ARTICLES THAT
TRIED TOO HARD, UNDERLINING THE ONES
THAT MADE YOU ACHE.
"GOD, I'D LOVE TO WRITE SOMETHING THIS
UNAPOLOGETIC," YOU SAID ONCE.
NOW I GET TO HELP SHAPE WHAT
UNAPOLOGETIC MEANS.
AND EVERY TIME I CUT A SENTENCE, I HEAR
YOUR VOICE SAY, "KEEP THE BLOOD. CUT THE
FLUFF."
I'VE BUILT MYSELF INTO SOMEONE I THINK
YOU MIGHT'VE LOVED—
IF I'D BEEN HIM WHEN IT STILL MATTERED.
AND MAYBE I'M STILL BUILDING.
BUT I WANTED YOU TO KNOW.
EVEN IF YOU NEVER READ THIS—
EVEN IF YOUR NUMBER CHANGED AND YOUR
LAST NAME ISN'T THE SAME—
I GOT THE JOB, MARE.
AND PART OF ME STILL HOPES YOU'D BE
PROUD. —S
PS. MARE... I'VE NEVER FUCKING USED A
'LEGAL PAD' IN MY LIFE MARE. YOU LIVE
HERE NOW. IN MY DESK DRAWER, ON A
FUCKING LEGAL PAD.

DEAR MARE,                    OCT 5 2007
I INTERVIEWED A WRITER TODAY.
 NEW TALENT. LATE TWENTIES. CONFIDENT,
BUT NOT COCKY.  SHE WALKED IN WEARING
BOOTS THAT LOOKED LIKE THEY'D SURVIVED
SOMETHING AND EYES THAT SAID SHE HAD, TOO.
SHE PITCHED ME A STORY ABOUT THE LIES WE
TELL IN LOVE.

 SOMETHING RAW. SOMETHING JAGGED.
SOMETHING I SHOULD'VE ASSIGNED ON THE
SPOT.
BUT I COULDN'T SPEAK FOR A SECOND.
BECAUSE HER VOICE—
GOD, MARE.  IT HAD YOUR RHYTHM. NOT
YOUR SOUND, NOT YOUR LILT.  YOUR
CADENCE.
 THE WAY YOU PAUSED LIKE PUNCTUATION WAS
A SACRED THING.

 THE WAY SHE LAUGHED AFTER SAYING
SOMETHING SHARP—LIKE SHE ALREADY
FORGAVE THE READER FOR FLINCHING. SHE SAT
ACROSS FROM ME AND SAID,
"I DON'T WANT TO WRITE WHAT'S PALATABLE. I
WANT TO WRITE WHAT BURNS."
AND I SWEAR, I ALMOST SAID YOUR NAME OUT
LOUD.

I DIDN'T, OF COURSE.

I NODDED. TOOK NOTES. SAID, "WE LIKE
BURN."
BUT SOMETHING IN ME WAS SHAKING.
BECAUSE FOR A MOMENT, I FELT LIKE I WAS
TALKING

TO THE GHOST OF THE WOMAN WHO FIRST
MADE ME BLEED FOR A SENTENCE.
WHO MADE ME BELIEVE WRITING COULD
UNDO A MAN AND STILL BE ART.
SHE LEFT AFTER TWENTY MINUTES.
I WATCHED HER WALK DOWN THE HALLWAY
AND DISAPPEAR.
AND I SAT THERE IN MY CHAIR, WONDERING
WHAT YOU WOULD'VE BECOME IF YOU HADN'T
LEFT ME.
OR WORSE—IF I'D DESERVED FOR YOU TO
STAY.
I THINK YOU WOULD'VE LIKED HER.
OR HATED HER, BECAUSE SHE REMINDS ME OF
YOU.
EITHER WAY, SHE LIT A FUSE IN THE ROOM I
THOUGHT I'D LOCKED SHUT.
YOU'RE STILL HERE, MARE.
EVEN IN OTHER PEOPLE'S MOUTHS.
EVEN IN STRANGERS' SYNTAX.
I STILL EDIT IN YOUR SHADOW.
—S

DEAR MARE,                          2/8/08
I DIDN'T THINK I'D WRITE TO YOU AGAIN.
I'VE SAID THAT BEFORE. WE BOTH KNOW WHAT
IT'S WORTH. BUT TONIGHT WAS DIFFERENT.
BECAUSE I DIDN'T THINK ABOUT YOU.
NOT ONCE.  NOT DURING THE DATE. NOT
DURING THE DRINKS.  NOT WHEN SHE
LAUGHED TOO LOUD OR LOOKED AT ME LIKE I
WAS WORTH THE WAIT.

AND NOT WHEN WE KISSED IN THE BACK OF THE
CAB.
 NOT WHEN SHE PULLED ME ONTO HER COUCH.
 NOT WHEN I PUT MY MOUTH ON HER
COLLARBONE AND FELT HER PULSE JUMP. NOT
EVEN WHEN I CAME.
NOT EVEN THEN. HER NAME'S VANESSA.

 MY BEST FRIEND SET US UP—SWORE WE'D
CLICK.
 WE DID. SHE'S SMART. DIRECT. WITTY WITHOUT
PERFORMING IT.  SHE MAKES EYE CONTACT LIKE
SHE'S TESTING FOR SMOKE.  AND WHEN SHE
CAME APART UNDER ME, IT FELT LIKE PROOF I
WASN'T DEAD.
IT WAS **GOOD**, MARE.

 NOT YOU. NOT THAT WILD, ACHING, BACK-OF-
THE-THROAT KIND OF HUNGER WE USED TO
DRAG OUT OF EACH OTHER.  BUT GOOD.

UNTIL 2:00 A.M.
UNTIL SHE ROLLED OVER AND TRACED HER
FINGER ALONG THE FACE OF MY WATCH.

THE ONE YOU PUT ON ME THE NIGHT YOU
LEFT. SHE ASKED WHERE I GOT IT. JUST A CASUAL
QUESTION. NOTHING LOADED.
BUT I FROZE. IT WAS LIKE SHE'D PUT HER
HAND ON YOUR THIGH INSTEAD OF MY WRIST.
LIKE SHE'D TOUCHED SOMETHING SACRED
WITHOUT KNOWING IT. AND SUDDENLY IT ALL
CAME BACK.
YOU. YOUR BREATH IN MY EAR.
YOUR FINGERS ON MY CHEST. YOUR SILENCE
IN THE MORNING. I COULDN'T BREATHE, MARE.
SHE WAS RIGHT THERE, BUT I FELT YOU.
I TOLD HER I WAS TIRED. ROLLED AWAY.
SHE'S ASLEEP NOW, WRAPPED IN MY SHEETS.
BUT I'M SITTING AT THE EDGE OF THE BED,
WRITING THIS WITH MY HANDS STILL SHAKING.
I WANTED TO FORGET. I THOUGHT MAYBE I HAD.
BUT THAT WATCH? IT'S NOT JEWELRY. IT'S YOU.
STILL TICKING. STILL COUNTING THE TIME
SINCE YOU WALKED AWAY. I DON'T KNOW IF
I'M ALLOWED TO MOVE ON. BUT I KNOW THIS
— EVEN WHEN I DO,
YOU'RE STILL THE THING THAT MAKES ME
FLINCH.
—S

Dear Mare,                                    October 2008

It's been about eight months, now

  I haven't written since February.
  I thought maybe I was done.

  Vanessa and I are still together.
   She's kind. Steady. The kind of woman
  who texts when she gets home and
  actually uses coasters.
   She knows what she wants.  She asks me
  what I want.  And most days, I answer like
  I believe I deserve the asking.

  It's easier now.  The grief doesn't gut
  me.
   I don't see your face in every stranger
  or choke on your name when someone
  says "Mare" like the ocean.
  But last night, I dreamed of you.
  You were sitting at my kitchen table,
  eating a peach like it was the only thing
  that mattered.
   Sunlight in your curls. That soft smirk
  on your mouth—the one that always
  meant trouble.
  You didn't say anything.
   You just looked at me like I still had
  time to tell the truth.

I WOKE UP SWEATING. HEART RACING.
 AND THAT ACHE—THE ONE THAT USED TO
HOLLOW ME OUT—
 IT WASN'T ALL THE WAY BACK.
 BUT IT WAS CLOSE.
I MADE COFFEE. VANESSA'S STILL ASLEEP.
 SHE SMELLS LIKE MY SHEETS NOW. SHE HUMS
WHEN SHE STIRS CREAM INTO HER CUP.

SHE'S THE KIND OF WOMAN I SHOULD'VE BEEN
GOOD FOR FROM THE START.
BUT YOU WERE THE STORM.
 AND STORMS DON'T SETTLE.
 THEY LIVE IN THE AIR AFTER, IN THE SILENCE
BETWEEN LIGHTNING AND BREATH.
**I'M TRYING, MARE.** I SWEAR I AM.
I'M REMEMBERING HOW TO WANT SOMETHING
THAT WON'T DESTROY ME.
 BUT I STILL FLINCH WHEN I HEAR PEACHES HIT
A CUTTING BOARD.

AND I THINK YOU'D LAUGH AT THAT.
 —S

DEAR MARE,                          FEB 6 2009
SHE ASKED ME WHERE WE WERE GOING.
AGAIN.
AND I SAT THERE—ON THE COUCH WE PICKED
OUT TOGETHER— AND COULDN'T SAY A DAMN
WORD.
NOT BECAUSE I DIDN'T CARE. NOT BECAUSE I
DIDN'T WANT TO TRY. BUT BECAUSE EVERY
VERSION OF "NEXT" I IMAGINED DIDN'T HAVE
HER IN IT.
IT WASN'T FAIR. NOT TO HER. NOT TO ME. IT
HAD BEEN A YEAR. SHE GAVE ME SPACE.
PATIENCE. WARMTH. SHE MADE PLANS LIKE SHE
BELIEVED I'D BE THERE TO SEE THEM
THROUGH.
AND I WANTED TO BELIEVE IT, TOO. BUT EVERY
TIME SHE ASKED FOR MORE, IT FELT LIKE
TRYING TO BUILD A FUTURE OVER A GRAVE I
HADN'T STOPPED VISITING. SO I TOLD HER I
NEEDED TIME.
SHE LOOKED AT ME, SMILED IN THAT SAD,
TIRED WAY PEOPLE DO WHEN THEY ALREADY
KNOW THE ENDING,
 AND SAID, "YOU'VE HAD TIME, SILAS. YOU
JUST HAVEN'T USED IT."
SHE WASN'T WRONG. THE BREAKUP HURT.
STILL DOES.
 STUNG LIKE PRESSING ON A BRUISE YOU
FORGOT WAS THERE.

BUT IT WASN'T YOU. IT WASN'T THAT.
WHEN YOU LEFT, IT FELT LIKE MY
SPINE WAS REMOVED WITHOUT
WARNING. LIKE I WAS WALKING
THROUGH THE WORLD WITH A HOLLOW
CORE AND NO LANGUAGE FOR PAIN.
THIS? THIS WAS A QUIET MERCY. A
MUTUAL RELEASE.
BUT IT MADE ME REALIZE SOMETHING
I DIDN'T WANT TO ADMIT: I'M NOT
HEALED MARE
 I'VE BEEN PUTTING A GODDAMN
BAND-AID ON A BLEEDING ARTERY,
 CALLING IT RECOVERY JUST BECAUSE I
DIDN'T SCREAM EVERY DAY ANYMORE.
BUT I'M STILL NOT WHOLE. AND NO
MATTER HOW MANY NAMES I SAY,
 YOURS IS THE ONLY ONE THAT STILL
ECHOES WHEN THE ROOM GOES QUIET.
—S

GET OUT
GET OUT
GET THE FUCK OUT OF
MY HEAD

IT'S GETTING WORSE,
MARE. SO MUCH FUCKING
WORSE. I FEEL LIKE I'M
CRAZY. WHO DOES THIS.
HOLDS ON TO SOMEONE
LIKE THIS. I WANT TO
GET YOU OUT OF MY
FUCKING HEAD)!

DEAR MARE,                    APRIL 2009

IT'S YOUR BIRTHDAY.
AND IT'S BEEN FIVE YEARS SINCE YOU LEFT.
AND EVEN NOW—I WONDER IF SOMEONE MADE
YOU COFFEE THIS MORNING.
 IF SOMEONE LIT A CANDLE IN A CAKE AND
KISSED YOUR CHEEK LIKE THEY EARNED IT.
 IF ANYONE CALLED YOU MARE.
I WONDER IF YOU FLINCHED.
 IF YOUR STOMACH TURNED.
 IF YOU THOUGHT OF ME FOR EVEN A SECOND.
I WENT LOOKING FOR YOU AGAIN.
 SPENT HOURS ONLINE, CHASING YOUR NAME
THROUGH SEARCH ENGINES LIKE A PRAYER I
KEEP MISSPELLING.
NOTHING.
 IT'S LIKE YOU DISAPPEARED.
 LIKE I DREAMED YOU, AND MY BODY NEVER
WOKE UP.
I WENT BY THE CAFÉ ON GRANT.
 TWICE.
SAT BY THE WINDOW WITH A BOOK I DIDN'T
READ.
 WAITED FOR CURLS. FOR HONEY SKIN. FOR
THAT WALK YOU USED TO HAVE WHEN YOU
DIDN'T CARE WHO NOTICED.

YOU NEVER CAME IN.
I EVEN WENT BACK TO THE CLUB.
THE GIRL WHO LOOKED LIKE YOU? SHE
WASN'T THERE.
I SAT THROUGH THREE HOURS OF MUSIC, OF
FLASHING

LIGHTS, OF WOMEN WHO TOUCHED ME WITHOUT
TOUCHING ANYTHING REAL.
AND I LEFT EMPTIER THAN I ARRIVED.
I'VE BECOME DESPERATE, MARE.
VANESSA WAS A DISTRACTION.
THIS MADE ME REALIZE THAT.
SHE WAS WARMTH, YES. BUT SHE WASN'T
FIRE.

THIS ISN'T ROMANTIC ANYMORE.
IT'S NOT POETIC.
IT'S NOT EVEN THE MAN YOU LEFT.
JUST A DESPERATE, HOLLOWED-OUT VERSION
OF HIM—
STILL SEARCHING THE WORLD FOR ONE PIECE
OF YOU.
AND I'M TIRED.
SO THIS IS MY LAST LETTER, MARIS.
NOT BECAUSE I DON'T STILL WANT YOU.
BUT BECAUSE I CAN'T LIVE LIKE THIS
ANYMORE.
YOU'RE IN EVERYTHING.
EVERY EDIT I MAKE.
EVERY STREET I TURN DOWN TOO FAST.
EVERY TIME SOMEONE SAYS "WAIT" IN A VOICE
THAT ALMOST SOUNDS LIKE YOURS.
YOU'RE IN MY MARROW.
AND I'M TIRED OF BREAKING MY OWN BONES
TO REACH YOU.
SO THIS IS IT.
THE LAST TIME I PUT PEN TO PAPER IN YOUR
NAME.
IF I SEE YOU AGAIN—IF YOU EVER SHOW UP IN
THIS LIFE OR THE NEXT—
I WILL LOVE YOU.
FULLY.
WITHOUT FEAR.
BUT I WON'T KEEP DYING IN THIS DRAWER.
HAPPY BIRTHDAY, MARE. GOODBYE.
—S

Jan/12/2016

DEAR MARIS

IT'S BEEN ALMOST SEVEN YEARS SINCE I
WROTE TO YOU.
 AND YET THIS PEN STILL KNOWS THE RHYTHM
OF YOUR NAME.
I WAS UNPACKING BOXES.
 MOVING AGAIN.
 NOT BECAUSE I HAD TO—BUT BECAUSE I
FINALLY BOUGHT LAND.
 I'M BUILDING A HOUSE.
I OPENED A BIN MARKED "OFFICE."
 HALF-FULL. A MIX OF NOTEBOOKS, DEAD
PENS, RECEIPTS FROM CITIES I BARELY
REMEMBER.
 AND THERE IT WAS—
 THE LEGAL PAD.
 THE ONE I TOLD YOU ABOUT IN THE LAST
LETTERS.
I SAT ON THE FLOOR AND READ EVERY WORD
LIKE THEY WEREN'T MINE.
 SOME OF THEM FELT LIKE SOMEONE ELSE
WROTE THEM.
 SOMEONE YOUNGER. ANGRIER. LOUDER.
 SOME OF THEM STILL FELT TOO TRUE. TOO
CLOSE.
 LIKE TIME DIDN'T TOUCH THEM AT ALL.
I HAVEN'T WRITTEN.
 BUT THAT DOESN'T MEAN I HAVEN'T MISSED
YOU.
 I DO.

EVERY MINUTE OF EVERY DAY.
BUT LIFE—LIFE FILLED UP AROUND THE
MISSING.
WORK KEPT ME MOVING.
I GOT TO TRAVEL. EVERYWHERE. PARIS.
SEOUL. CAPE TOWN. TOKYO.
ALWAYS FOR STORIES. ALWAYS CHASING
TRUTH.
SOMETIMES IT HELPED.
SOMETIMES I'D BE IN A CROWDED MARKET OR
WALKING DOWN A NEON-LIT ALLEY AND
THINK,
"SHE WOULD'VE LOVED THIS."

I WENT TO CULINARY SCHOOL.
 DIDN'T TELL ANYONE AT THE MAGAZINE. IT WAS A NIGHT PROGRAM, TUCKED BETWEEN DEADLINES AND EXHAUSTION. BUT I FINISHED.
I COOK NOW. REALLY COOK.
THERE'S SOMETHING ABOUT FEEDING PEOPLE THAT FEELS HONEST. NO EDITS. NO METAPHORS.
 JUST... HEAT AND HANDS AND HUNGER.
 YOU WOULD'VE CALLED IT PRIMAL.
 YOU WOULD'VE KISSED ME WITH SALT STILL ON MY LIPS AND ASKED ME TO RUIN YOU WITH DESSERT.
WOMEN HAVE COME AND GONE.
 SOME STAYED A WHILE. NONE MADE IT PAST THE ECHO.
NOT BECAUSE I'M BROKEN.
 I'M NOT. BUT BECAUSE THEY WANTED A VERSION OF ME I'VE NEVER BEEN ABLE TO SUSTAIN.
I'M NOT THE MAN YOU LEFT.
 AND I'M NOT THE MAN WHO WROTE THAT LAST LETTER, EITHER. BUT I'M CLOSER TO THE MAN I WISH I'D BEEN.
I'M UP FOR ANOTHER PROMOTION.
 EXECUTIVE EDITOR THIS TIME.
 FEELS LIKE A CROWN I DIDN'T ASK FOR.
 BUT MAYBE I'M READY TO WEAR IT NOW.
I'VE BEEN GETTING MORE TATTOOS.
 THOUGHT I'D STOP AFTER THREE.
 I WAS WRONG. I'M THINKING FULL SLEEVES. MAYBE A PIECE ON MY RIBS NEXT.

ONE OF THEM— IS A MARE. NOT A LITERAL
PORTRAIT. MORE LIKE A SKETCH.
 FERAL AND WILD-EYED, MID-REAR, HOOVES
CATCHING WIND.
 I TOLD THE ARTIST I WANTED IT TO FEEL LIKE
SOMETHING THAT WOULD NEVER BE TAMED.
HE DELIVERED. SOMETIMES I CATCH MYSELF
TRACING IT ABSENTMINDEDLY.
 LIKE I'M STILL TRYING TO FIND YOU IN THE
INK.
 I DON'T KNOW WHY I'M WRITING THIS NOW.
 MAYBE I NEEDED TO MARK THE MOMENT.
 MAYBE FINDING THE PAD BROKE SOMETHING
OPEN.
 OR MAYBE I NEEDED TO REMEMBER WHAT IT
FELT LIKE TO TALK TO SOMEONE WHO MADE
ME FEEL LIKE EVERY WORD MATTERED.
 I WON'T PRETEND THIS IS A FRESH WOUND.
 IT'S NOT.  IT'S SCARRED OVER.
 BUT THAT DOESN'T MEAN I DON'T STILL PRESS
IT WHEN IT RAINS.
 I DON'T KNOW WHERE YOU ARE, MARE.
 OR WHO YOU BECAME.  BUT I HOPE—
 I HOPE SOMEONE IS FEEDING YOU WELL.
 I HOPE SOMEONE IS MAKING YOU LAUGH IN
THE DARK.  I HOPE YOU NEVER STOPPED
WRITING.
 AND I HOPE YOU'VE FORGIVEN ME IN SOME
QUIET CORNER OF YOUR SPIRIT I'LL NEVER
TOUCH AGAIN.
 —SILAS

5/12/16

DEAR MARE,

I GOT THE JOB. EDITOR-IN-CHIEF.
THEY HANDED ME THE TITLE, SHOOK MY
HAND, TOLD ME I'D EARNED IT— AND ALL I
COULD THINK WAS: I WISH YOU COULD SEE
ME NOW. NOT FOR THE PRESTIGE. NOT FOR
THE PAYCHECK. BUT BECAUSE I FINALLY
BECAME
THE MAN YOU USED TO DESCRIBE BETWEEN
KISSES.
I MOVED INTO THE HOUSE LAST WEEK. IT'S
QUIET. MODERN. GOOD BONES. BUT I BUILT
IT FOR YOU.
DO YOU REMEMBER THAT NIGHT—
YOU WERE STRADDLING ME ON THE FLOOR
OF THE STUDIO, MY SHIRT HALF-BUTTONED,
AND YOU TOLD ME ABOUT YOUR DREAM
HOUSE?
YOU WANTED A VIEW OF THE LAKE. SO YOU
COULD SIT OUT THERE AND WRITE.
YOU SAID YOU WANTED IT TO BE PEACEFUL.
HONEST. SOMEWHERE YOU DIDN'T HAVE TO
LIE TO YOURSELF IN.

YOU WANTED A LONG HALLWAY WITH ART
LINING THE WALLS, AND ONE GIANT,
UNAPOLOGETIC PORTRAIT OF A MARE—YOUR
MARE— RIGHT IN THE CENTER.
YOU WANTED A GOURMET KITCHEN. AND FOR
ME TO LEARN HOW TO COOK FOR YOU.
"REAL ADULT FOOD," YOU SAID,
WHISPERING IT INTO MY NECK LIKE A
SECRET RECIPE.
I REMEMBER EVERY WORD.
AND I BUILT ALL OF IT.
EVERY DAMN DETAIL. EVEN THE MARBLE
BACKSPLASH—

THE ONE YOU SAID MADE A KITCHEN FEEL
  "LIKE A WOMAN WHO DOESN'T APOLOGIZE
FOR TAKING UP SPACE."
I BUILT THIS HOME IN YOUR IMAGE.
AND I'VE WALKED THROUGH IT EVERY DAY
THIS WEEK
  WONDERING WHAT IT WOULD FEEL LIKE
  TO HAND YOU A GLASS OF WINE IN THAT
KITCHEN.
  TO FUCK YOU AGAINST THOSE COUNTERS.
  TO WAKE UP BESIDE YOU WITH THE LAKE
STEAMING IN THE MORNING SUN.
I GOT THE JOB. I GOT THE HOUSE. I GOT
EVERYTHING I THOUGHT I WANTED.
AND NONE OF IT MEANS A THING WITHOUT YOU
IN IT.
THE RING? IT'S YOURS. I DESIGNED IT A YEAR
AGO,
  WHILE THE HOUSE WAS STILL STUDS AND
SCAFFOLDING.
I FELT RIDICULOUS WHEN THE DESIGNER
CONGRATULATED ME ON THE ENGAGEMENT.
  I DIDN'T CORRECT HER.
  I JUST NODDED,
IMAGINING THE DAY I'D SEE YOU AGAIN—
  IN A CAFÉ, CROSSING A STREET,
  STANDING IN FRONT OF ME LIKE NO TIME HAD
PASSED AT ALL.
SO, I PLAN.
  AND I WAIT.
  AND I LIVE IN THE SHADOWS OF YOUR
MEMORY.

THIS LIFE.
THIS HOUSE.
THIS RING.
IT'S ALWAYS BEEN YOURS, AND I SHOULD
HAVE WAITED FOR YOU IN THIS LIFE.
MAYBE I STILL AM.
I DON'T KNOW IF I'LL EVER GET TO ASK
YOU.
BUT IF THE DAY EVER COMES—
IF YOU WALK THROUGH THAT FRONT DOOR
LIKE YOU NEVER LEFT—
I'LL BE WAITING. I'LL DROP TO MY KNEES.
I'LL ASK WITH MY WHOLE SOUL.
I'LL PUT THIS ON YOUR FINGER. AND CALL IT
HOME.
YOURS IN EVERY ROOM,
SILAS

DEAR MARE,                                        AUG 18

SHE LEFT. ANDRIENNE. NO YELLING. NO
SLAMMED DOORS. NO DRAMATICS.
SHE WALKED OUT OF THIS HOUSE LIKE IT
NEVER BELONGED TO HER, AND IN A WAY—IT
DIDN'T.
BECAUSE IT ALWAYS BELONGED TO YOU.
SHE FOUND THE BOX. THE LETTERS. YOU.
I DIDN'T HIDE THEM. NOT WELL, ANYWAY.
I KEPT THEM TUCKED IN A DRAWER BESIDE
THE BED. THE ONE SHE USED TO PUT HER
JEWELRY IN WHEN SHE STAYED THE NIGHT.
MAYBE I WANTED HER TO FIND THEM. MAYBE I
NEEDED SOMEONE ELSE TO CONFIRM WHAT I
ALREADY KNEW. THAT YOU NEVER REALLY
LEFT.
SHE SAT ACROSS FROM ME ON THE COUCH,
QUIET, COMPOSED, AND ASKED, "WHO IS
MARE?"
AND I DIDN'T LIE. I TOLD HER THE TRUTH.
YOU WERE THE WOMAN I FELL IN LOVE WITH
BEFORE I KNEW WHAT IT MEANT TO STAY. THE
WOMAN I'VE BEEN WRITING TO FOR OVER TEN
YEARS.
THE WOMAN I STILL DREAM ABOUT WHEN THE
HOUSE CREAKS LATE AT NIGHT.
SHE SAID, "THAT'S NOT LOVE, SILAS. THAT'S
OBSESSION." BUT IT ISN'T.
IT'S DEVOTION.

YOU CRACKED SOMETHING OPEN IN ME, MARE.
YOU HELD IT. SHAPED IT. NAMED IT.
AND WHEN YOU LEFT, I TRIED TO CLOSE THE
LID—BUT IT DIDN'T SEAL.
I DIDN'T ASK HER TO STAY.
SHE DESERVED MORE THAN WHAT I COULD
GIVE HER.
BECAUSE NO MATTER HOW MANY DINNERS WE
SHARED, HOW MANY TIMES SHE LAUGHED AT
MY DRY JOKES, HOW MANY SUNDAY MORNINGS
SHE FOLDED INTO MY SIDE—
SHE NEVER FOUND HER WAY INTO MY BONES
LIKE YOU DID.
SHE'S GONE NOW.
AND THE FIRST THING I DID AFTER THE DOOR
SHUT...
WAS WRITE YOU.
BECAUSE I DON'T KNOW HOW TO STOP.
BECAUSE I DON'T WANT TO STOP.
BECAUSE I'M STILL YOURS.
SILAS

DEAR MARE,                          APRIL 2024


I CAN'T FUCKING BREATHE. IT'S YOU. IT'S
YOU. IT'S THE FIRST REAL GLIMPSE I'VE HAD
IN NEARLY TWENTY GODDAMN YEARS AND I
RECOGNIZED YOUR VOICE BEFORE THE END OF
THE FIRST LINE. NOT YOUR NAME. NOT YOUR
FACE.
 YOUR VOICE. YOU DIDN'T SIGN IT. DIDN'T
NEED TO. YOU UNDRESSED ME ON THE PAGE
LIKE YOU NEVER STOPPED KNOWING HOW.
LIKE YOUR HANDS STILL REMEMBER THE
GEOGRAPHY OF MY RIBS AND MY RUIN.
YOU WROTE THAT SCENE LIKE YOU REMEMBER
WHAT I SOUND LIKE WHEN I BREAK.
 YOU WROTE THAT SCENE LIKE IT HAPPENED.
LIKE IT FUCKING HAPPENED.
I READ IT. THEN I READ IT AGAIN. THEN I SHUT
MY OFFICE DOOR AND READ IT WITH MY
FUCKING HAND.
I CAME WITH YOUR NAME IN MY MOUTH,
MARE.
 NOT SOFTLY. NOT REVERENTLY. LIKE A MAN
STARVING. LIKE IT HURT. LIKE IT WAS MINE.
YOU UNDID ME IN THREE PAGES.
MY BODY HASN'T RESPONDED LIKE THAT IN
YEARS. NOT WITH THAT KIND OF DESPERATION.
 NOT WITH THAT KIND OF ACHE. NOT WITH THAT
NEED TO MARK SOMETHING. TO BITE.
 TO CLAIM.

YOU DIDN'T WRITE THAT FOR A STRANGER.
YOU WROTE THAT FOR ME. DIDN'T YOU?
DIDN'T YOU?
GOD, I'M SHAKING. I'M SITTING HERE WITH
THE STORY OPEN AND I CAN'T FUCKING MOVE.
YOU'RE IN MY OFFICE. YOU'RE IN MY
BLOODSTREAM. YOU'RE IN MY TEETH. YOU'RE
IN MY FUCKING MARROW AGAIN.
AND I DON'T KNOW IF I WANT TO RUN OR
FALL TO MY KNEES.
IF YOU'RE BACK—IF YOU'RE REALLY BACK— I
DON'T KNOW HOW I'M SUPPOSED TO SURVIVE
IT.
BECAUSE I'M NOT THE SAME MAN YOU LEFT.
BUT MY BODY? IT NEVER STOPPED WAITING
FOR YOU.
—S

I KNEW IT WAS YOU BEFORE I FINISHED THE FIRST PARAGRAPH.

THE CADENCE. THE ACHE BETWEEN THE LINES. THE WAY YOU HELD BACK JUST ENOUGH, BUT NOT QUITE. THE MIRROR ROOM. THE MARE IN THE REFLECTION. YOUR MOUTH PARTING LIKE YOU WERE TRYING TO REMEMBER WHAT IT WAS LIKE TO BE WORSHIPPED.

FUCK MARE.

I READ IT A HUNDRED TIMES.

THEN I CLOSED MY OFFICE DOOR AND READ IT AGAIN IN THE DARK.

I UNZIPPED MY PANTS, GRIPPING MYSELF WITH SHAKING HANDS AND SAYING YOUR NAME OUT LOUD. ONCE.

SOFT.

LIKE IT MIGHT ECHO TOO LOUD IN A ROOM THAT NEVER KNEW THE SOUND OF YOU.

AND THEN I CAME—HARD. FAST. LIKE MY BODY HAD BEEN WAITING FOR PERMISSION.

I HADN'T SAID YOUR NAME LIKE THAT IN YEARS.

IT BURNED LIKE GOSPEL.

AFTER, I STARED AT THE CEILING FOR AN HOUR. THE WATCH ON MY WRIST TICKING TOO LOUD, LIKE IT REMEMBERED, TOO.

I DON'T KNOW WHAT WRECKED ME MORE—YOUR WORDS, OR THE REALIZATION THAT THE WOMAN WHO ONCE BEGGED ME TO WRITE ABOUT HER HAD WRITTEN HERSELF INTO THE WORLD WITHOUT ME.

I USED TO THINK I KNEW WHAT LOSS FELT
LIKE.
BUT THIS?
READING YOUR TRUTH AS A STRANGER,
KNOWING I WASN'T THE ONE YOU SENT IT TO—
BUT KNOWING YOU WROTE IT FOR ME ANYWAY?
THAT GUTTED ME.
YOU SAID IN THE STORY THAT HE SAW YOU IN
THE MIRROR AND DIDN'T LOOK AWAY.
I NEVER DID, MARE.
I NEVER LOOKED AWAY.
EVEN WHEN I SHOULD'VE.
THE MEMORY OF YOUR SMILE, YOUR CARAMEL
KISSED SKIN.
THE WAY THE CURLS OF YOUR HAIR FELT
WRAPPED AROUND MY FINGERTIPS.
THE WAY YOU SHOOK WHEN YOU CAME.
THE SOUND YOU MADE WHEN I KISSED YOUR
SPINE.
IT ALL CAME BACK.
LIKE A WAR I THOUGHT I'D SURVIVED BUT
NEVER WALKED AWAY FROM.
YOU WROTE ABOUT THE MIRROR, BUT MARE—
BUT I'M THE ONE WHO SHATTERED.
AND NOW THAT I'VE FOUND YOUR VOICE
AGAIN,
I DON'T THINK I CAN PRETEND NOT TO HEAR
IT.
NOT ANYMORE.
YOURS STILL,
SILAS

DEAR MARE,

I THINK I FOUND YOU.
I'M NOT SURE YET. I DON'T EVEN KNOW IF YOU'LL RESPOND. BUT I SENT THE TEXT.
IS IT YOU? MARE?
THAT'S ALL I WROTE. JUST THOSE FIVE WORDS. AND MY HANDS STILL HAVEN'T STOPPED SHAKING.
I WENT DIGGING. NOT THROUGH YOUR SOCIAL —NONE OF THAT EVER WORKED. BUT I REACHED OUT TO A COUPLE OF YOUR OLD PUBLISHING CONTACTS. PEOPLE YOU ONCE MENTIONED. PEOPLE WHOSE NAMES STUCK LIKE BREADCRUMBS IN MY MEMORY.
ONE OF THEM STILL WORKS AT A SMALL PRESS IN SAN FRANCISCO. SHE PAUSED WHEN I SAID YOUR NAME. SAID, "SHE GOES BY HARTLEY NOW." HARTLEY.
IT CAUGHT IN MY THROAT. MARIS HARTLEY.
I DON'T KNOW WHY IT HURT. IT'S JUST A NAME. A DETAIL. BUT IT FELT LIKE WATCHING A DOOR CLOSE AND OPEN AT THE SAME TIME.
SHE GAVE ME THE NUMBER. SAID SHE SHOULDN'T. SAID SHE WASN'T EVEN SURE IT WAS STILL YOURS.
I DIDN'T CARE.
I

SAT WITH IT FOR TWENTY MINUTES, STARING
AT THE DIGITS LIKE THEY MIGHT BURN ME. I
WROTE THE MESSAGE THREE TIMES. DELETED
IT. REWROTE IT. DELETED AGAIN. THEN I SENT
IT.
JUST ENOUGH HOPE TO MAKE ME FEEL LIKE
I'M GOING TO BE SICK. I DON'T KNOW WHAT
I'LL DO IF YOU DON'T ANSWER. AND I DON'T
KNOW WHAT I'LL DO IF YOU DO.
BUT I KNOW I HAD TO TRY.
BECAUSE YOU WROTE ME INTO THE MIRROR
ROOM. AND NOW I'M TRYING TO WALK
THROUGH IT.
CALL IT CLOSURE. CALL IT MADNESS.
CALL IT LOVE THAT NEVER FUCKING DIED.
I'M HERE. AND I'M WAITING.
—S

DEAR MARE,                    APRIL 2024

MARE, IT'S YOU. YOU RESPONDED.
FUCK, MARE. I DON'T KNOW WHAT
I'M DOING. WHILE I HADN'T FULLY
MOVED ON, I'D SETTLED INTO LIFE. A
CAREER. A RHYTHM. BUT READING
THAT STORY—YOU WROTE ME BACK
INTO EXISTENCE. NICK. THE NAME
YOU USED THE LAST TIME YOU WROTE
A STORY ABOUT US. THE WATCH. THE
ENGRAVING. THE TATTOOS. BEING
SEEN AFTER ALL THESE YEARS? FUCK,
MARE. THIS ISN'T ME READING INTO
THINGS. YOU FUCKING WROTE TO ME.
WHY? WHAT WAS THE REASON? AND
NOW I'M FUCKING HOOKED. YOU
AGREED TO MEET WITH ME TODAY. I
HAVEN'T SLEPT. I'VE PACED THE
FLOOR. I'VE HAD THREE GLASSES OF
WHISKEY. I'VE COME. TWICE. AND I'M
STILL WRECKED. I'M FUCKING FERAL.
AND IN A MATTER OF HOURS, I'M
GOING TO BE IN THE SAME ROOM WITH
YOU AGAIN AFTER TWENTY FUCKING
YEARS. GOD HELP US BOTH. —S

DEAR MARE,                                    APRIL 2024
I'M STILL IN THE CAR. STILL PARKED. STILL
GRIPPING THE STEERING WHEEL LIKE IT'S THE
ONLY THING KEEPING ME FROM FALLING INTO
THE NIGHT.
YOU WERE THERE. **REALLY THERE.**
I SAW IT HIT YOU TOO.
THE WAY YOUR BREATH CAUGHT THE MOMENT
YOU LOOKED UP AND SAW ME.
 THE WAY YOUR FINGERS FIDGETED UNDER
THE TABLE WHEN YOU THOUGHT I WASN'T
WATCHING.
 THE WAY YOU CROSSED AND UNCROSSED YOUR
LEGS LIKE YOU WERE TRYING TO GROUND
YOURSELF.
YOU LOOKED SO FUCKING BEAUTIFUL, MARE.
 FULL.
 CURVIER THAN I REMEMBERED—IN A WAY
THAT MADE MY BREATH HITCH AND MY MOUTH
GO DRY.
GOD, YOU LOOKED LIKE YOU'D BEEN LOVED
AND HURT AND HEALED AND UNDONE AND
REBUILT—
 AND ALL I WANTED TO DO WAS MEMORIZE
THE VERSION OF YOU I GOT TONIGHT.
I FLIRTED. **OF COURSE I DID.**

I TEASED YOU JUST TO SEE IF I COULD STILL
MAKE YOU FLUSH. AND WHEN I DID—WHEN I
SAW THAT LITTLE PINK BLOOM UNDER YOUR
CHEEKBONES—I SWEAR TO GOD, IT TOOK
EVERYTHING IN ME NOT TO REACH ACROSS THE
TABLE AND TOUCH YOUR FACE LIKE IT
BELONGED TO ME.
I WORE THE WATCH.  YOU SAW IT. **AND I SAW
YOU SEE IT.**
YOU BLINKED A LITTLE TOO LONG.
 YOU BIT THE INSIDE OF YOUR CHEEK LIKE
YOU USED TO WHEN YOU DIDN'T WANT TO SAY
SOMETHING YOU'D REGRET.
 AND I SAID WHAT I COULD—TOLD YOU I
SEARCHED YOUR NAME EVERY YEAR.
 TOLD YOU EVERYTHING AFTER YOU WAS JUST
WEATHER.
BUT THE TRUTH IS?
YOU'RE STILL THE STORM.
AND NOW I DON'T KNOW WHAT TO DO WITH
MYSELF.
 BECAUSE I SAW IT, MARE.
I SAW YOU FEEL IT TOO.
YOU TRIED TO BE CAREFUL.
 BUT YOUR BODY GAVE YOU AWAY.
AND I'M SITTING HERE IN THE DARK, STILL
TASTING THE SPACE BETWEEN US—
 TERRIFIED AND CERTAIN THAT I'M ALREADY
YOURS AGAIN.
IF TONIGHT WAS A BEGINNING...
 GOD HELP US BOTH.
 —S

MARE, I CAME THINKING ABOUT YOU THE SECOND I GOT HOME. HARD. FAST. NO HESITATION. IT WASN'T EVEN ABOUT GETTING OFF. IT WAS ABOUT RELEASING SOMETHING THAT'S BEEN BURIED FOR TWENTY YEARS. AND I KNOW YOU DID TOO. I COULD SEE IT ALL OVER YOU—IN THE FLUSH RISING UP YOUR NECK, IN THE WAY YOUR THIGHS PRESSED TOGETHER UNDER THE TABLE, IN THE WAY YOUR BREATH CAUGHT WHEN YOUR EYES DROPPED TO WHERE I WAS HARD AND UNDENIABLE. AND FUCK, WHEN I KISSED YOUR FACE? THAT GENTLE, REVERENT KISS— YOUR KNEES BUCKLED. YOU REACHED FOR ME LIKE INSTINCT. LIKE WE HADN'T BEEN APART FOR TWO DECADES. LIKE I STILL BELONGED TO THE SPACE BETWEEN YOUR BREATH AND YOUR SKIN. IT WAS LIKE SOMETHING BURST INSIDE ME. NOT LUST. NOT HOPE. SOMETHING DEEPER. SOMETHING I THOUGHT I'D BURIED UNDER A CAREER AND A THOUSAND NIGHTS ALONE. I HAVEN'T FELT UNDONE LIKE THIS IN YEARS. I HAVEN'T FELT ALIVE IN YEARS. ALL THIS TIME, I'VE BEEN SLEEPWALKING—THROUGH AIRPORTS, DEADLINES, MEETINGS, OTHER BODIES, OTHER BEDS. BUT YOU? YOU CRACKED SOMETHING OPEN AGAIN. AND NOW EVERYTHING FEELS LOUDER. MORE REAL. BUT HERE'S

THE PART THAT'S EATING ME: YOU'RE
MARRIED. YOU HAVE A DAUGHTER. YOU'VE
BUILT A LIFE—STABLE, FULL, ANCHORED.
AND I'M NOT JEALOUS, MARE. I SWEAR I'M
NOT. I'M JUST HAUNTED BY THE FACT THAT
YOU WERE ABLE TO BUILD SOMETHING
WHILE I'VE BEEN STUCK IN ORBIT—
CIRCLING YOUR MEMORY LIKE A FUCKING
SATELLITE, NEVER LANDING, NEVER
MOVING ON, JUST WATCHING FROM A
DISTANCE AS YOU BECAME SOMEONE ELSE'S
HOME. I DON'T KNOW WHAT ANY OF THIS
MEANS. I JUST KNOW THAT MY BODY STILL
REMEMBERS YOURS. AND MY HANDS STILL
ACHE TO HOLD EVERYTHING I ONCE LET GO.
YOU BROUGHT ME BACK TO LIFE TODAY. AND
NOW I DON'T KNOW WHAT THE FUCK TO DO
WITH THAT. —S

APRIL 18 2024

DEAR MARE,

I WROTE TO YOU TONIGHT. NOT IN THIS NOTEBOOK. NOT IN A DRAWER. NOT TO A GHOST.
I WROTE TO YOU ON QUILL. WHERE YOU COULD SEE ME. REALLY SEE ME.

FOR YEARS, I'VE BEEN THROWING WORDS INTO THE ETHER—SCRATCHING YOU INTO PAGES NO ONE ELSE WOULD READ.

BUT TONIGHT WAS DIFFERENT. TONIGHT I POURED OUT EVERYTHING I'VE BEEN THINKING FOR YEARS. EVERYTHING I'VE WANTED.

EVERYTHING I'VE BURIED UNDER WORK AND WHISKEY AND WOMEN WHO NEVER FELT LIKE HOME. AND FOR THE FIRST TIME IN TWO DECADES, I DIDN'T FEEL LIKE I WAS UNRAVELING INTO SILENCE. I FELT HEARD.
IT WAS MY ONLY SAVING GRACE. PUTTING IT OUT THERE, KNOWING YOU WOULD READ IT. NOT HOPING. **KNOWING**. AND IT GAVE ME A STRANGE KIND OF CALM. LIKE MY CHEST FINALLY STOPPED CAVING IN.

# THE FIRST QUILL LETTER I WROTE...

YOU LOOKED EXACTLY HOW I REMEMBER,
AND NOTHING LIKE I DESERVE.
I TOLD MYSELF I WOULDN'T SAY ANYTHING
WHEN I SAW YOU.
I TOLD MYSELF I'D BE COOL—
PROFESSIONAL. POLITE.
BUT THERE YOU WERE, STANDING IN FRONT
OF ME WITH THAT SAME MOUTH THAT RUINED
ME,
AND I CAN'T EVEN PRETEND I FORGOT THE
TASTE OF IT.
GOD, MARE.
TWENTY YEARS AND I STILL REMEMBER THE
WAY YOUR BODY ARCHED WHEN I WHISPERED
"MINE."
I STILL WAKE UP WITH YOUR NAME IN MY
MOUTH LIKE A BRUISE I KEEP PRESSING.
YOU WANT TO SIT IN MY WORLD? THEN LET
ME SHOW YOU WHERE I'VE KEPT YOU.
IN MY OFFICE DRAWER, UNDER THE
TRAVEL RECEIPTS AND RANDOM JOTTED
NOTES,
IS A PICTURE OF YOU.

I WEAR THE WATCH. DAILY. THE ONE YOU GAVE
ME. THE ONE I SWORE I WOULDN'T WEAR.
BUT I DO. I CAN'T REMEMBER THE LAST TIME I
TOOK IT OFF OTHER THAN TO SHOWER.
 AND I LIE TO MYSELF. I SAY IT'S FOR
CLOSURE. THAT I WEAR IT TO MOVE ON.
 BUT THE TRUTH?
 I WEAR IT BECAUSE IT STILL SMELLS LIKE
YOUR SKIN WHEN I HOLD IT TOO CLOSE.
 YOU CAME BACK INTO MY LIFE LIKE A
SENTENCE I NEVER GOT TO FINISH.
 AND NOW I WANT TO SAY EVERY WORD.
 I WANT TO SAY—
 YOU RUINED ME, MARE.
 YOU REMADE ME, MARE.
 YOU STILL FUCKING OWN ME, MARE.
 YOU KNOW WHAT I REMEMBER? THE WAY
YOUR LAUGH USED TO CURL AROUND THE
ROOM LIKE SMOKE.
 HOW YOU'D TILT YOUR HEAD WHEN YOU
WERE ABOUT TO LIE—
 NOT TO ME.
 TO YOURSELF. TO THE RULES.
 TO THE ACHE THAT TOLD YOU THIS WAS ALWAYS
MORE THAN A FLING.
 AND I PLAYED ALONG WELL, DIDN'T I?
 PLAYED THE MARRIED MAN WITH RESTRAINT.

THE EDITOR WITH BOUNDARIES. THE LOVER
WITH A LEASH.
BUT YOU? YOU WERE WILD.
YOU WERE A FEVER I KEPT FEEDING WITH
DENIAL.
AND NOW—
NOW YOU'RE BACK,
AND SEEING YOU MADE MY HANDS SHAKE LIKE
THE FIRST TIME I TRACED YOUR HIPBONE WITH
MY MOUTH.
YOU ONCE TOLD ME THAT I DIDN'T GIVE YOU
THE SOFT VERSION OF ME...
I DIDN'T GIVE YOU THE RAW. THE POETRY.
YOU WANT POETRY?
THEN HERE:
YOU WERE THE RED IN MY GRAYSCALE LIFE,
THE HEAT IN MY WINTER BREATH,
THE YES I MAY HAVE WHISPERED INTO THE
NECK OF EVERY NO.
I MAY HAVE KISSED OTHER MOUTHS.
BUT YOURS?
YOURS IS THE PRAYER I NEVER FINISHED.
DO YOU WANT MORE?
BECAUSE I'LL GIVE IT TO YOU.
IN VERSE, IN VOICE, IN VELVET. IN SWEAT.
IN SILENCE, BROKEN ONLY BY THE WAY YOU
SAY MY NAME WHEN YOU'RE NO LONGER
PRETENDING YOU DON'T STILL WANT THIS.
WANT ME.
DON'T MOVE, MARE.
STAY IN THE WORLD I BUILT FOR YOU.
STAY WITH ME.

# THE SECOND QUILL LETTER...

I JUST WOKE UP FROM A DREAM. I WAS
STANDING OUTSIDE OF YOUR WINDOW,
BEGGING YOU TO LET ME IN.
 BUT INSTEAD, YOU MADE ME WATCH WHILE
YOU FUCKED HIM... YOUR HUSBAND. MOANED
HIS NAME AS YOUR BODY CLENCHED AROUND
HIM.
 BUT YOUR EYES? YOUR EYES STAYED FOCUSED
ON ME AS HE FUCKED YOU.
 I WOKE UP IN LITERAL PAIN, MARE.
 MAYBE IT'S JEALOUSY.
 NO...NOT JEALOUSY. MARE, IT FUCKING
WRECKED ME.
 BECAUSE I KNOW THAT SOUND.
 I KNOW THE WAY YOUR MOANS TURN
DESPERATE WHEN YOU'RE CLOSE,
 HOW YOUR BREATH CATCHES JUST BEFORE YOU
FALL APART.
 AND THE THOUGHT THAT HE GETS TO HEAR IT—
 GETS TO FEEL THE QUAKE IN YOUR BODY,
 WHILE IT IS MY NAME ECHOING INSIDE YOUR
HEAD?
 YES.
 I'M FUCKING JEALOUS.
 NOT OF THE SEX. NOT OF HIS HANDS.
 BUT OF THE FACT THAT HE GETS TO BE IN THE
ROOM WHEN I AM THE ONE INSIDE OF YOU.

I WONDER IF HE NOTICES.
THE DISTANCE IN YOUR EYES.
THE TREMBLE THAT ISN'T FOR HIM.
THE WAY YOUR BODY OPENS, BUT YOUR SOUL
STAYS LOCKED IN MY MEMORY.
TELL ME...
DOES YOUR THIGHS CLENCH THE WAY THEY
USED TO AROUND MY SHOULDERS?
DOES YOUR BREATH STILL CATCH LIKE YOU
ARE DROWNING IN THE TASTE OF ME?
DO YOU CLOSE YOUR EYES AND PICTURE THE
WATCH YOU GAVE ME,
TICKING BESIDE YOUR BED AGAIN?
YOU CAN FUCK HIM. YOU CAN TASTE HIM.
YOU CAN LET HIM TAKE YOUR BODY.
BUT WHEN YOUR PLEASURE HAS MY NAME
STITCHED INTO ITS SEAMS?
YOU'RE STILL MINE, MARE.
AND I'LL BE WAITING FOR THE DAY YOU
MOAN "SILAS" WITHOUT BITING IT BACK.

# THE THIRD QUILL LETTER...

YOU KNOW, I USED TO WRITE LETTERS TO YOU.
NEVER SENT THEM OF COURSE.
DIDN'T NEED TO.
THE ACT OF WRITING WAS ENOUGH TO MAKE
YOU FEEL REAL AGAIN.
I'D WRITE,
"DEAR MARE,
I SAW SOMEONE TODAY WITH YOUR HAIR,
BUT SHE DIDN'T HAVE YOUR FIRE.
SHE DIDN'T BITE HER LIP LIKE SHE WAS
HOLDING BACK A MOAN OR A MEMORY."
I'D WRITE,
"YOU ONCE TOLD ME I TASTED LIKE BOURBON
AND BAD TIMING.
YOU WERE RIGHT.
BUT YOU NEVER SAID YOU DIDN'T LIKE THE
TASTE."
I'D WRITE,
"I STILL WANT YOU.
NOT THE VERSION OF YOU THAT LEFT,
BUT THE ONE THAT STAYED IN EVERY LINE
I'VE EVER EDITED,
EVERY STORY I'VE EVER TOUCHED."
AND WHEN I WASN'T WRITING YOU?

I WAS TRYING NOT TO FIND YOU IN OTHER
WOMEN. FAILED EVERY TIME.
BECAUSE NONE OF THEM KNEW HOW TO
COMMAND A ROOM WITH A GLANCE.
NONE OF THEM HAD A VOICE THAT MADE MY
KNEES WEAK BEFORE YOU EVEN SAID MY
NAME.
GOD, MARE, DO YOU KNOW WHAT IT DID TO
ME? TO BE IN LOVE WITH SOMEONE I COULD
NEVER FULLY HAVE?
TO LIVE IN THE AFTERMATH OF YOU?
YOU WERE THE AFFAIR THEY WARNED MEN
ABOUT IN WHISPERED LOCKER ROOMS AND
LATE-NIGHT CONFESSIONS.
YOU WERE THE LESSON. THE LEGEND.
THE WOMAN I SHOULD'VE FORGOTTEN BUT
BUILT AN ALTAR TO INSTEAD. AND NOW?
YOU'RE BACK IN MY WORLD. SO I'LL GIVE
YOU POETRY. I'LL GIVE YOU PRAISE.
**I'LL GIVE YOU THE TRUTH WITH MY
HANDS AND MY MOUTH AND MY
GODDAMN MARROW IF YOU ASK.**
BUT YOU HAVE TO LET ME. SAY THE WORD,
MARE. SAY ANYTHING. OR SAY NOTHING.
I'LL STILL BE HERE, WRITING YOU INTO THE
DARK, UNTIL DAWN ASKS IF I'VE EVER LOVED
ANYONE ELSE. AND I'LL TELL HER NO.
**BECAUSE HOW DO YOU LOVE ANOTHER
WOMAN WHEN YOU'RE STILL BLEEDING
FROM THE ONE WHO CALLED HERSELF A
STORM?**

THE FOURTH QUILL LETTER
THE NIGHT YOU LEFT. YOU DIDN'T KNOW I
HEARD YOU. IT WAS BARELY A WHISPER. I
DON'T EVEN KNOW IF YOU REALIZED THE
WORDS CAME OUT OF YOUR MOUTH...LIKE AN
INTERNAL THOUGHT THAT ACCIDENTALLY
ESCAPED.
"DID YOU EVER REALLY EVEN LOVE ME?"
BEFORE I COULD ANSWER, RUN AFTER YOU,
GRAB YOUR FACE AND TELL YOU... YOU WERE
GONE.
GOD, MARE.
YOU HAVE NO IDEA HOW MANY NIGHTS I'VE
REGRETTED THAT DAY. HOW I WANTED TO
COME FIND YOU. BUT I WASN'T THE MAN YOU
DESERVED, NOT THEN.
BUT I SWORE IF I EVER GOT THE CHANCE, I'D
TELL YOU EXACTLY WHAT I WANTED TO TELL
YOU THEN. AND EVERY ANSWER I REHEARSED
FEELS TOO SMALL NOW THAT YOUR VOICE IS
SHAKING IN MY MEMORY AGAIN.
SO...MARE. DID I LOVE YOU?
NO.
I BURNED FOR YOU. I WORSHIPPED YOU IN
SILENCE.
I REWROTE MY WHOLE GODDAMN LIFE
AROUND THE SHAPE OF YOUR ABSENCE.
YOU WEREN'T A FLING. YOU WEREN'T AN
AFFAIR. YOU WEREN'T EVEN A MISTAKE.

YOU WERE THE MOMENT THAT SPLIT ME IN
TWO:
BEFORE MARE. AFTER MARE.
I LOVED YOU SO FULLY; IT TERRIFIED ME.
BECAUSE YOU WEREN'T EASY.
YOU WEREN'T SOFT.
YOU WERE THIS HOLY, IMPOSSIBLE THING THAT
MADE ME QUESTION EVERYTHING I THOUGHT I
WAS—
A HUSBAND, A WRITER, AN ARTIST, A MAN
WHO HAD "ENOUGH."
YOU LOOKED AT ME LIKE I WAS MORE.
AND I WANTED TO BE.
I WANTED TO RISE TO THE VERSION OF
MYSELF THAT YOUR EYES SAW.
AND WHEN YOU LEFT?
I DIDN'T JUST LOSE YOU. I LOST HIM.
SO YES. I LOVED YOU. I STILL DO.
AND NOT THE WAY PEOPLE MEAN WHEN THEY
SAY THAT YEARS LATER.
NOT THE NOSTALGIC, SAFE KIND OF LOVE.
I MEAN THE KIND THAT STILL MAKES MY BODY
HUM WHEN I HEAR YOUR NAME.
THE KIND THAT RUINS EVERY WOMAN WHO
ISN'T YOU.
THE KIND THAT MAKES IT IMPOSSIBLE TO
FORGET THE TASTE OF YOUR SKIN BENEATH THE
INK OF YOUR THIGHS.
I LOVED YOU, MARE.

AND IF YOU ASKED ME TO PROVE IT NOW, I'D
DO IT WITHOUT BLINKING.
SAY THE WORD. SAY MY NAME.
AND I'LL SHOW YOU
WHAT TWENTY YEARS OF BURIED DEVOTION
FEEL LIKE
WHEN IT FINALLY GETS TO BREATHE.
YOU HAVE NO IDEA WHAT IT DOES TO ME.
HEARING MY NAME IN YOUR MOUTH AFTER
ALL THIS TIME. LIKE YOU NEVER STOPPED
SAYING IT.
LIKE IT'S BEEN THERE, WAITING, BEHIND
EVERY SIGH AND EVERY SENTENCE THAT
NEVER MADE IT TO THE PAGE.
MARE—
IF I COULD TOUCH YOU NOW,
I WOULDN'T START WITH YOUR SKIN.
I'D START WITH YOUR MEMORY.
WITH EVERY PLACE I'VE HAUNTED YOU IN
DREAMS.
EVERY LINE YOU WROTE WHERE YOU
THOUGHT YOU WERE ALONE,
BUT I WAS THERE—BETWEEN THE COMMAS.
WATCHING. WANTING.
WAITING.

AND IF YOU ASKED ME TO PROVE IT NOW, I'D DO IT
WITHOUT BLINKING.
SAY THE WORD. SAY MY NAME.
AND I'LL SHOW YOU
WHAT TWENTY YEARS OF BURIED DEVOTION FEEL LIKE
WHEN IT FINALLY GETS TO BREATHE.
YOU HAVE NO IDEA WHAT IT DOES TO ME.
HEARING MY NAME IN YOUR MOUTH AFTER ALL THIS TIME
LIKE YOU NEVER STOPPED SAYING IT.
LIKE IT'S BEEN THERE, WAITING, BEHIND EVERY SIGH AND
EVERY SENTENCE THAT NEVER MADE IT TO THE PAGE.
MARE—
IF I COULD TOUCH YOU NOW,
I WOULDN'T START WITH YOUR SKIN.
I'D START WITH YOUR MEMORY.
WITH EVERY PLACE I'VE HAUNTED YOU IN DREAMS.
EVERY LINE YOU WROTE WHERE YOU THOUGHT YOU WERE
ALONE,
BUT I WAS THERE—BETWEEN THE COMMAS.
WATCHING. WANTING.
WAITING.
NOW YOU'RE HERE. YOU'RE REAL.
AND I DON'T GIVE A DAMN HOW LONG I'VE LIVED
WITHOUT YOU—
I WOULD TRADE EVERY MINUTE OF SURVIVAL FOR ONE
NIGHT OF TRUTH.
SO ASK ME AGAIN.
ASK ME IF I STILL LOVE YOU.
ASK ME IF I REMEMBER THE SOUND THAT YOU MADE
WHEN YOU CAME FOR THE FIRST TIME IN MY ARMS.
ASK ME, MARE…
BECAUSE I'VE GOT TWENTY YEARS OF THE WORD 'YES'
LODGED IN MY THROAT, AND I NEED YOU TO FUCKING
TAKE IT.

I BLED FOR YOU TONIGHT, MARE. IN A WAY I HAVEN'T DONE IN YEARS. I NEEDED YOU TO READ EVERY BREATHE THAT WAS FOR YOU, EVERY WHISPER, EVERY NUANCE BETWEEN THE LINES.

I'D JUST LAID DOWN. BODY EXHAUSTED. HEART WIDE OPEN. AND THEN MY PHONE LIT UP. YOUR MESSAGE. FOUR WORDS. I NEED TO SEE YOU. I DIDN'T THINK. DIDN'T HESITATE. I SENT YOU THE PIN STILL TASTING YOUR NAME IN THE BACK OF MY THROAT. STILL WONDERING IF THIS IS REAL. IF YOU'RE REALLY ON YOUR WAY. IF I'M ABOUT TO HOLD THE WOMAN I'VE ONLY EVER ACHED FOR. COME TO ME, MARE. COME RUIN ME. COME RESURRECT ME.

—S

**MARE,**　　　　　　　　　　　APRIL 19 2024

WHEN YOU GOT OUT OF THE CAR, I SWEAR
I'D NEVER SEEN YOU LOOK SO BROKEN. NOT
ANGRY. NOT TIRED. NOT GUARDED. GONE.
YOU LOOKED LIKE SOMEONE WHO'D RUN OUT
OF PLACES TO HIDE HER PAIN. AND WHEN I
SAW YOUR FACE, I KNEW—I WASN'T THERE
TO TALK. I WASN'T THERE TO SEDUCE. I
WASN'T EVEN THERE TO EXPLAIN. I WAS
THERE TO HOLD SPACE FOR YOUR COLLAPSE.

I'M SORRY FOR SHOWING UP THE WAY I DID.
UNINVITED. UNAPOLOGETIC. BUT I DIDN'T
HAVE A CHOICE. NOT AFTER YOUR TEXT. NOT
AFTER I KNEW YOU WERE ALONE. I
WOULD'VE BURNED THE WHOLE FUCKING
CITY DOWN TO GET TO YOU. AND THE SECOND
I SAW YOU, I KNEW WHAT YOU NEEDED
MORE THAN ANYTHING WAS TO BE ALLOWED
TO BREAK. TO FALL APART WITHOUT ANYONE
ASKING YOU TO HOLD IT TOGETHER. AND
GOD, MARE—YOU DID. YOU BROKE. YOU
SHATTERED. YOU WEPT LIKE THE SOUND WAS
A LANGUAGE ONLY YOUR BODY
REMEMBERED.

AND I SAT NEXT TO YOU IN THAT TUB, WASHING YOUR HAIR WITH FINGERS THAT HAVE ONLY EVER WANTED TO WORSHIP YOU, AND I TRIED NOT TO FALL APART MYSELF. BUT YOUR TEARS? THEY NEARLY CUT ME IN HALF. IT WAS THE MOST BEAUTIFUL AND PAINFUL THING I'VE EVER WITNESSED. I'VE SEEN YOU WILD. I'VE SEEN YOU HIGH ON PLEASURE AND DRENCHED IN LAUGHTER AND DRUNK ON POWER. BUT I HAVE NEVER SEEN YOU SO UNSHIELDED. YOU LET ME IN. NOT TO FIX YOU. NOT TO HOLD YOU UP. JUST... TO BE THERE. AND I SWEAR, MARE—THAT MOMENT CHANGED ME. AGAIN.

BUT MARE, I HAVE TO BE FULLY HONEST. THAT WAS THE HARDEST THING I'VE EVER DONE IN MY LIFE.

YOUR BODY IS MORE BEAUTIFUL THAN I REMEMBER. THE CURVES TIME GIFTED YOU. THE SOFTNESS SHARPENED BY EXPERIENCE. YOU MOVED LIKE GRIEF AND DESIRE WERE BRAIDED TOGETHER IN YOUR BONES. AND THE SOUND YOU MADE—WHEN I PRESSED MY THUMB INTO THE ARCH OF YOUR FOOT—MARE, I WOULD HAVE DROWNED IN A THOUSAND SEAS OVER THE PAST TWENTY YEARS TO HEAR THAT SOUND AGAIN.

THAT WAS MY BREAKING POINT. THAT WAS WHEN I HAD TO WALK AWAY. HAD TO GRIP THE EDGE OF THE TUB AND BREATHE LIKE I WAS KEEPING MYSELF ALIVE WITH NOTHING BUT WILLPOWER.

THEN I MET YOUR DAUGHTER. FUCK, MARE. SHE'S YOU. REINCARNATE. SAME FIRE. SAME GRIT. SAME WAY OF LOOKING SOMEONE STRAIGHT IN THE EYE LIKE SHE'S ALREADY FIGURED THEM OUT. AND I STOOD ACROSS FROM HER AND THOUGHT—OF COURSE YOU BUILT HER. OF COURSE SHE'S MADE OF YOUR STEEL AND SOUL. OF COURSE SHE BURNS LIKE YOU. AND I WANTED TO TELL HER. EVERYTHING. HOW YOU ONCE LIT UP MY WHOLE GODDAMN WORLD. HOW YOU STILL DO. BUT I DIDN'T. BECAUSE THIS STORY IS STILL UNFOLDING. AND I DON'T KNOW YET WHAT PART I GET TO PLAY.
- S

MARE,
I GOT A TEXT FROM YOUR PHONE. IT BUZZED ONCE. I SAW YOUR NAME AND FELT THAT FAMILIAR PUNCH TO THE STERNUM. BUT IT WASN'T YOU. IT WAS ANGIE.

HEY SILAS, THIS ISN'T MARIS, IT'S ANGIE, THE DAUGHTER. THE ONE YOU WERE A LITTLE AFRAID OF EARLIER. YOU CAN ADMIT IT. HEY! COME TO DINNER. NEED TO TALK. 8. BRING WINE.

I READ IT TWICE. THREE TIMES. LAUGHED OUT LOUD, ALONE IN MY KITCHEN, HAND OVER MY MOUTH LIKE I WASN'T SURE IF IT WAS A JOKE OR A DOOR SWINGING WIDE OPEN.

AFRAID OF HER? YEAH. A LITTLE.

SHE SAW THROUGH ME WITHIN THIRTY SECONDS. HAD MY NUMBER BEFORE I'D SAID MY OWN NAME.

SHE'S SHARP. TOO SHARP. SHE'S YOU, MARE.
NOT JUST IN FIRE AND GRIT, BUT IN INSTINCT.
SHE KNEW I WASN'T HERE FOR SMALL TALK.
AND NOW SHE'S INVITING ME BACK LIKE SHE
ALREADY KNOWS I'LL SAY YES. BECAUSE I
WILL. OF COURSE I FUCKING WILL.

BECAUSE SOMETHING'S HAPPENING HERE.
SOMETHING REAL. AND EVEN IF IT TERRIFIES
ME—EVEN IF I STILL DON'T KNOW WHAT PART
I'M SUPPOSED TO PLAY—I WANT TO SIT AT
YOUR TABLE. I WANT TO BRING WINE. AND
STORIES. AND THE KIND OF SILENCE THAT
MEANS SOMETHING. I'LL BE THERE. —S

APRIL 19 2024

MARE,

ANGELA MONROE. ANGELA MONROE.
I CAN'T GET THAT SHIT OUT OF MY HEAD,
MARE. ALL THIS TIME—ALL THIS FUCKING TIME
—I THOUGHT YOU'D FORGOTTEN ABOUT ME.
THAT YOU'D MOVED ON, ERASED ME, REBUILT
YOUR WORLD SILAS-FREE. AND YOU GAVE HER
A PART OF ME. SECRETLY. QUIETLY. LIKE A
TOAST IN THE DARK BETWEEN LOVERS ACROSS
GALAXIES. LIKE YOU WHISPERED IT INTO HER
SKIN WHEN NO ONE ELSE WAS LISTENING.

ANGELA. MIDDLE NAME MONROE.

AND MARE—GOD. I'LL WORK UP THE COURAGE
TO ASK THE QUESTION ONE DAY. SOON. BUT
NOT NOW. NOT YET. BECAUSE HERE'S THE
TRUTH I'M STILL SHAKING WITH—SHE DOESN'T
LOOK LIKE ME. SHE DOESN'T NOT LOOK LIKE
ME EITHER. AND MY HEART ACHES AT THE
THOUGHT—THAT SHE MIGHT BE MINE. THAT I
MIGHT HAVE MISSED HER ENTIRE LIFE. THAT I
WAS OUT IN THE WORLD CHASING GHOSTS
WHILE MY BLOOD WAS LIVING UNDER YOUR
ROOF.

I DON'T KNOW HOW TO HOLD THAT YET. I DON'T KNOW HOW TO BREATHE WITH THAT POSSIBILITY IN MY CHEST. BUT I WILL. I SWEAR I WILL. BECAUSE TONIGHT? TONIGHT WAS THE BEST NIGHT OF MY ENTIRE FUCKING EXISTENCE. SHE WAS HILARIOUS AND SHARP AND RELENTLESS. SHE CALLED ME OUT WITHOUT HESITATION. SHE ASKED QUESTIONS I WASN'T READY TO ANSWER AND SOMEHOW DIDN'T MAKE ME FEEL SMALL FOR FUMBLING. SHE'S YOURS. AND SHE MIGHT BE MINE. AND WHETHER THAT'S BLOOD OR ACCIDENT OR FATE—THANK YOU. THANK YOU FOR GIVING ME A PIECE OF YOUR LIFE AND GIVING HER A PIECE OF ME. GOD, I LOVE YOU. —S

MARE,                                    APRIL 27 2024

I CAN STILL SMELL YOU ON MY SKIN.
THAT'S PROBABLY A FUCKED-UP WAY TO
START A LETTER, BUT I PROMISED MYSELF I
WOULDN'T LIE. NOT TO YOU. NOT TO ME.
NOT EVEN TO THE GODDAMN PAPER.
SO, HERE'S THE TRUTH:
I LOST CONTROL TONIGHT.
AFTER MEETING ANGIE, I TOLD MYSELF I
WOULDN'T TOUCH YOU. THAT IF YOU CAME
NEAR ME, I'D BE DECENT. RESPECT YOUR
LIFE. RESPECT YOUR MARRIAGE AND FAMILY.
RESPECT THE VERSION OF YOU THAT WALKED
AWAY FROM ME ALL THOSE YEARS AGO AND
NEVER LOOKED BACK.
BUT THEN YOU SAID YOU WERE STILL MINE.
AND IT BROKE SOMETHING IN ME.
I'VE REPLAYED THAT SENTENCE A HUNDRED
TIMES ALREADY, LIKE MAYBE IF I REWIND IT
ENOUGH, IT WON'T CRACK ME OPEN THE
SAME WAY. IT STILL DOES.
YOU SAID YOU'RE STILL MINE, AND THEN
YOU LOOKED AT ME LIKE I HADN'T ALREADY
FAILED YOU ONCE.

I SHOULDN'T HAVE TOUCHED YOU.
I SHOULDN'T HAVE PINNED YOU AGAINST THAT CAR.
SHOULDN'T HAVE MADE YOU COME LIKE YOU BELONGED TO ME.
BUT FUCK, MARE.
YOU DO.
YOU ALWAYS DID.

AND I'VE SPENT TWENTY YEARS BUILDING A LIFE THAT LOOKS GOOD ON PAPER WHILE CHOKING ON EVERY VERSION OF YOU I COULDN'T HAVE.
I THOUGHT IF I LEFT YOU STANDING IN THAT DRIVEWAY—IF I DIDN'T FUCK YOU RIGHT THERE WITH MY WHOLE HEART UNRAVELING—I'D BE THE BETTER MAN.
TURNS OUT I'M NOT.
I'M STILL THE SAME MESS WHO WRITES LETTERS HE NEVER SENDS. WHO CARVES HORSES INTO WOOD AND NAMES THEM AFTER THE GIRL WHO RUINED HIM.
I DON'T KNOW WHAT HAPPENS NEXT.
I DON'T KNOW IF YOU'LL READ THIS.
BUT IF YOU DO...
I HOPE YOU KNOW I WOULD'VE WAITED A LIFETIME FOR THAT ONE SENTENCE.
AND I HOPE ONE DAY, YOU'LL SAY IT AGAIN.
AND MEAN IT WITH YOUR WHOLE BODY.
YOURS,
SILAS

MARE, I WOKE UP FUCKING THE AIR. NOT DREAMING—MOVING. GRINDING INTO NOTHING WITH YOUR NAME AT THE BACK OF MY THROAT AND YOUR GHOST RIDING ME LIKE SMOKE. LIKE SIN. LIKE SALVATION. LIKE I WAS NEVER MEANT TO SURVIVE YOU. I CAME...
HALF-AWAKE AND FULLY WRECKED. SHEETS TANGLED. BOXERS SOAKED. HEART POUNDING LIKE I'D BEEN RUNNING TOWARD YOU IN MY SLEEP AND DIDN'T MAKE IT IN TIME.

YOU'VE ALWAYS BEEN UNDER MY SKIN, MARE. BUT LAST NIGHT? THAT WAS THE BREAK IN THE DAM. THAT WAS THE RELAPSE. I'VE BEEN ~~MARIS-FREE~~ FOR TWENTY YEARS. OR SO I TOLD MYSELF. KEPT MY HANDS BUSY. KEPT MY MOUTH FULL OF DISTRACTION. TOLD MYSELF THE DRAWER WAS SHUT. THE STORY OVER. BUT LAST NIGHT IN THAT DRIVEWAY— WHEN YOU TOUCHED ME LIKE WE NEVER STOPPED, WHEN YOUR BREATH HIT MY JAW LIKE A PRAYER YOU COULDN'T FINISH— SOMETHING BROKE... **IN ME. IN TIME.**

THIS MORNING, I'M SHAKING. BECAUSE I'M
ASHAMED. BECAUSE I KNOW NOW. THERE IS NO
VERSION OF ME THAT DOESN'T WANT YOU. NO
DECADE CAN DULL IT. NO DISTANCE CAN BURY
IT. NO SILENCE CAN CAUTERIZE THIS THING
THAT STILL MOANS YOUR NAME IN THE DARK.

LAST NIGHT WAS A MISTAKE IN HOW I HANDLED
YOU, HANDLED THE WANT. BUT. IT WAS THE
TRUTH RESURFACING. AND I DON'T WANT TO
BE SOBER FROM YOU ANYMORE. —S

MAY 14,

MARE

IT'S BEEN A WEEK SINCE THAT NIGHT. AND I
HAVE FOUGHT MYSELF EVERY SINGLE DAY NOT
TO REACH OUT. NOT TO DRIVE TO YOU. NOT TO
FALL ON MY KNEES AT YOUR DOOR AND ASK
YOU TO FUCKING TELL ME TO STOP.

BECAUSE THERE IS NO VERSION OF THIS STORY
THAT ENDS WELL FOR ANYONE. I KNOW THAT.
GOD, I KNOW IT. BUT I DON'T KNOW WHAT I'M
DOING WITH MYSELF ANYMORE. I'M WALKING
AROUND THIS SHRINE I BUILT FOR YOU—THIS
HOUSE. THESE WALLS. EVEN THIS BODY. FUCK,
EVEN MY HAIR. YOU USED TO ASK ME TO
GROW IT OUT. I ALWAYS SAID NO. SAID IT
WASN'T ME. SAID I LIKED IT SHORT, CLEAN,
MANAGEABLE. BUT LOOK AT ME NOW. TWO
DECADES LATER, STILL TRYING TO BECOME THE
MAN I WAS TOO FUCKING PROUD TO BE WHEN
YOU NEEDED ME MOST.

I'VE SPENT YEARS COLLECTING PUZZLE PIECES. A LITTLE MORE TENDERNESS HERE. A LITTLE MORE PATIENCE THERE. A BETTER LISTENER. A BETTER COOK. A BETTER FUCKING MAN. ALL BUILDING TOWARD SOMEONE WHO COULD LOVE YOU BETTER. SOMEONE WHO COULD DESERVE YOU. I BUILT HIM. AND THEN I FUCKED IT. I FUCKED IT. AND NOW I SIT HERE, HATING MYSELF MORE THAN I HAVE IN YEARS.

BECAUSE I THOUGHT I'D GROWN. I THOUGHT I WAS READY. BUT ALL I AM IS WRECKAGE IN NICE CLOTHES. ALL I AM IS THE MAN WHO LET YOU WALK OUT ONCE AND MAY HAVE DONE IT AGAIN. I'M NOT ASKING FOR ANYTHING IN THIS LETTER. I DON'T EVEN KNOW IF YOU'LL READ IT. BUT I HAD TO SAY IT. BECAUSE SILENCE ISN'T KEEPING ME SAFE. IT'S KILLING ME. —S

MARE, YOU'RE ASLEEP BESIDE ME.
HAIR DAMP AT THE ROOTS. BREATH EVEN. SKIN
STILL HUMMING FROM EVERYTHING WE DID TO
EACH OTHER LAST NIGHT. AND I STILL FEEL
LIKE I'M DREAMING.
YOU TOLD ME. YOU TOLD ME ABOUT ANGIE.
AND BABY—SHE'S MINE. MY DAUGHTER. MY
FLESH AND BLOOD. MY FIRE AND GRIT AND
SARCASM AND SHARP-EYED REBELLION. SHE'S
OURS. AND I DON'T KNOW HOW TO HOLD THAT.
NOT ALL AT ONCE. NOT WITHOUT CRUMBLING
UNDER THE WEIGHT OF WHAT I MISSED.
BUT SOMEHOW—HERE IN THIS ROOM, WITH
YOU SLEEPING BESIDE ME, AND THE ACHE IN
MY THIGHS STILL STITCHED WITH YOUR NAME—
IT DOESN'T FEEL LIKE PUNISHMENT. IT FEELS
LIKE RESURRECTION. ALL THIS TIME, I
THOUGHT I WAS CHASING A GHOST. BUT IT TURNS
OUT I WAS CHASING MY FAMILY. AND TONIGHT?
I FOUND BOTH OF YOU.

YOU WERE EVERYTHING. EVERY SOUND YOU MADE. EVERY WAY YOU OPENED TO ME. EVERY WORD YOU DIDN'T SAY—BECAUSE YOU DIDN'T HAVE TO. YOUR BODY KNEW MINE. STILL. AFTER TWENTY YEARS. YOU TOUCHED ME LIKE NOTHING HAD BEEN LOST, AND I TOUCHED YOU LIKE I WAS BEING FORGIVEN. WE DIDN'T JUST FUCK. WE DIDN'T JUST MAKE LOVE. WE CAME HOME.

AND NOW I'M SITTING HERE, WRITING THIS IN THE DARK, KNOWING THAT FOR THE FIRST TIME IN MY ENTIRE FUCKING LIFE, I AM EXACTLY WHERE I'M SUPPOSED TO BE. WITH YOU. WITH HER. WITH EVERYTHING WE BUILT WITHOUT REALIZING IT. THANK YOU. FOR TRUSTING ME. FOR LETTING ME BACK IN. FOR NOT LETTING TWENTY YEARS OF SILENCE KILL THE THING WE NEVER STOPPED BEING. I LOVE YOU. I LOVE HER. I LOVE US. —S

MARE, YOU'RE GONE AGAIN. BACK TO YOUR PLACE. BACK TO YOUR RHYTHM. BACK TO THE SPACE THAT HELD YOU FOR THE YEARS I DIDN'T. AND I GAVE YOU THE BOX. ALL OF IT. THE NOTEBOOKS. THE LOOSE PAGES. THE LETTERS I NEVER THOUGHT YOU'D SEE. THE ONES WRITTEN IN GRIEF, IN LUST, IN RAGE, IN SILENCE.

IT'S OUT OF MY HANDS NOW. AND I'M STILL WRITING. I DON'T KNOW WHY. MAYBE IT'S RITUAL NOW. MAYBE IT'S CEREMONY. MAYBE IT'S THE ONLY WAY I KNOW HOW TO STAY CLOSE TO YOU WHEN YOUR BODY ISN'T NEAR MINE. BUT MARE—I'M SHAKING. BECAUSE I KNOW YOU'RE GOING TO READ THEM. ALL OF THEM. AND I DON'T KNOW WHAT YOU'LL FIND. A MAN TRYING. A MAN FAILING. A MAN CRAWLING BACK TO THE MEMORY OF YOU WITH BLOODY KNEES AND NO MAP.

BUT I HOPE—GOD, I HOPE—YOU SEE THE LOVE.
EVEN WHEN IT WAS MESSY. EVEN WHEN IT WAS
SELFISH. EVEN WHEN IT WAS WRITTEN IN PAST
TENSE PAIN.
AND TODAY—I HAD LUNCH WITH ANGIE. WE
WENT TO THE CAFÉ. GRANT STREET. CAN YOU
BELIEVE THAT? THE PLACE WHERE I USED TO SIT
WITH A BOOK I COULDN'T READ, PRAYING THE
DOOR WOULD OPEN AND YOUR SHADOW WOULD
SPILL IN BEHIND IT. AND NOW I SAT THERE WITH
OUR DAUGHTER.

SHE BROUGHT A PHOTO ALBUM. PAGES OF HER
GROWING. SMILING. FALLING OFF SWINGS AND
CLIMBING TREES AND GRADUATING WITH FIRE IN
HER EYES. AND MARE—SHE LOOKS LIKE YOU.
BUT FUCK, SHE ALSO LOOKS LIKE ME. WE SAT
THERE FOR HOURS. TALKING. LAUGHING.
FILLING IN TWENTY YEARS IN SLOW SIPS OF ICED
TEA AND MEMORIES I NEVER HAD.

SHE TOLD ME SHE FELT IT. RIGHT AWAY. THAT THERE WAS A BUZZ WHEN WE TALKED AT THE DINNER TABLE. SOMETHING IN HER KNEW. SHE TOLD ME JAY WOULD ALWAYS BE HER DAD. THAT HE EARNED THAT. THAT HE WAS GOOD AND KIND AND PRESENT. BUT THEN SHE LOOKED AT ME—DEAD IN THE EYE—AND SAID, "THAT DOESN'T MEAN I DON'T WANT YOU TO BE, TOO."

MARE, I NEARLY BROKE RIGHT THERE. I'VE NEVER BEEN SO GRATEFUL OR SO HUMBLED. NOT IN MY ENTIRE LIFE. AFTER LUNCH, WE WALKED THE BOARDWALK. GOT ICE CREAM LIKE SHE WAS FIVE. I'VE NEVER KNOWN JOY LIKE THAT. NOT THE KIND THAT SITS IN YOUR CHEST LIKE WARMTH INSTEAD OF WEIGHT. AND MAYBE —JUST MAYBE—THIS IS WHAT FORGIVENESS LOOKS LIKE. NOT THE DRAMATIC KIND. NOT THE LOUD, CINEMATIC KIND. THE KIND THAT FEELS LIKE WALKING BESIDE YOUR DAUGHTER ON A THURSDAY AFTERNOON, AND REALIZING YOU DIDN'T MISS EVERYTHING. NOT ALL OF IT. SOMEHOW... YOU GAVE ME THE MOST IMPORTANT PART. —S

MARE, YOU CRIED IN MY ARMS LAST NIGHT.
LIKE THE WEIGHT OF TWO DECADES FINALLY
GAVE WAY, AND THE ONLY THING LEFT TO DO
WAS FALL.
AND I CAUGHT YOU. LIKE I WAS ALWAYS
SUPPOSED TO. LIKE MY ARMS REMEMBERED
THE SHAPE OF YOUR SORROW. YOU TOLD ME
ABOUT THAT DAY. THE DAY I SAW YOU,
SWOLLEN WITH OUR DAUGHTER, AND WALKED
AWAY. AND IT SHATTERED YOU. AND GOD,
MARE—HEARING IT FROM YOUR MOUTH WAS
WORSE THAN ANY NIGHTMARE I'VE EVER
MADE FOR MYSELF.
I THOUGHT I WAS PUNISHING MYSELF ALL
THESE YEARS. BUT NOTHING I IMAGINED
COMPARED TO THE SOUND OF YOUR VOICE
BREAKING AS YOU SAID, "WHY DIDN'T YOU
COME FOR ME."
I SHOULD'VE RUN TO YOU. I SHOULD'VE
DROPPED TO MY KNEES IN THE STREET. I
SHOULD'VE DONE EVERYTHING DIFFERENTLY.
BUT LAST NIGHT—YOU LET ME HOLD YOU.
YOU LET ME HOLD THE PAIN. AND WHEN YOU
FINALLY STOPPED SHAKING, YOU PULLED
YOUR HAND FROM THE BLANKET AND SHOWED
ME THE RING.

YOU FOUND IT. YOU KEPT IT. **YOU WORE IT.** EVEN BEFORE I ASKED THE QUESTION AGAIN. BECAUSE YOU **KNEW.** YOU FELT THE WORDS STILL HANGING IN THE AIR. YOU KNEW I STILL MEANT **EVERY FUCKING SYLLABLE.**

AND WHEN YOU LOOKED AT ME—EYES RAW, CHEEKS WET, VOICE LIKE SMOKE CURLING AROUND THE EDGE OF FORGIVENESS—YOU SAID: "YES." AND I HAVE NEVER LOVED YOU MORE THAN I DID IN THAT MOMENT.

YOU DIDN'T SAY IT WITH FANFARE. YOU DIDN'T NEED MUSIC OR KNEELING OR MOONLIGHT. YOU SAID IT LIKE THE EARTH FINALLY STOPPED SPINNING JUST LONG ENOUGH FOR US TO CATCH UP. YOU SAID YES LIKE YOU WERE ALWAYS GOING TO. AND MARE—I SWEAR TO YOU, THIS TIME I'M NEVER GOING ANYWHERE. YOU, ME, ANGIE—US. I STILL CAN'T BELIEVE I GET TO HAVE YOU. BUT I DO. AND I WILL. FOREVER.
—S

MARE, TODAY'S LUNCH WITH YOU, ANGIE, AND JAY WAS AWKWARD AS **FUCK.**

LIKE, VIOLENTLY AWKWARD. IF IT WEREN'T FOR ANGIE, I THINK I WOULD'VE CRAWLED UNDER THE TABLE AND USED IT LIKE AN UMBRELLA TO GET THE FUCK OUT OF DODGE. BRUTAL. LIKE, PALPABLE SILENCE AND SECONDHAND SHAME BRUTAL.
BUT IT HAD TO BE DONE. AND, GOD—THANK YOU FOR NOT SUGARCOATING IT. FOR NOT TRYING TO MAKE IT CUTE. FOR LETTING IT BE HARD. BECAUSE IT WAS. AND THEN... IT WASN'T. THEN IT WAS GOOD. THEN GREAT. THEN SOMEHOW IT WAS AMAZING.

JAY WAS GRACIOUS IN THAT WAY THAT MAKES ME FEEL LIKE SHIT AND GRATEFUL ALL AT ONCE.
AND ANGIE? SHE TURNED THE WHOLE FUCKING THING AROUND LIKE SHE ALWAYS DOES. PULLED LAUGHTER OUT OF THIN AIR. BRIDGED A TWENTY-YEAR GAP LIKE IT WAS NOTHING MORE THAN A DINNER COURSE.

AND I SAT THERE THINKING—I CAN'T BELIEVE WE'RE HERE. I CAN'T BELIEVE THIS IS US. THREE MONTHS FROM A WEDDING. OUR WEDDING. MARE—I HAVE NEVER BEEN THIS FUCKING HAPPY IN MY LIFE.

IT DOESN'T FEEL LIKE A DREAM. IT FEELS EARNED. IT FEELS LIKE THE WHOLE WORLD FELL APART JUST TO REBUILD ITSELF INTO THIS.

YOU. ME. HER. EVEN HIM. THIS TWISTED, HEALING, IMPERFECT CONSTELLATION WE'RE BUILDING—I WOULDN'T TRADE IT FOR ANYTHING. —S

MARE—PREGNANT. FUCKING **PREGNANT.** AND I'M NOT EVEN SCARED. **NOT ONE GODDAMN BIT.** THIS ISN'T A MISTAKE. THIS ISN'T AN ACCIDENT. THIS IS FATE. THIS IS THE UNIVERSE SCREAMING **FINALLY.**

THIS IS THE STARS LINING UP, THE TIMELINES SHIFTING, THE MAPS REDRAWING THEMSELVES BECAUSE WE FOUND OUR WAY BACK. THIS IS YOU. THIS IS ME. AND BABY MAKES FIVE. ANGIE. JAY. YOU. ME.

THIS BABY. OUR FUCKING LIFE, MARE. AND I CAN'T WAIT. I CAN'T WAIT TO HOLD THIS PIECE OF US. TO KISS YOUR BELLY. TO FEEL TINY FEET KICK UNDER MY HAND AND KNOW THAT WE MADE THIS. YOU GAVE ME BACK MY PAST. YOU GAVE ME MY DAUGHTER. AND NOW YOU'RE GIVING ME THIS TOO? I DON'T KNOW WHAT I DID TO DESERVE IT, BUT I SWEAR TO GOD, I'LL SPEND THE REST OF MY LIFE LOVING EVERY MINUTE OF OUR YEARS APART OUT OF OUR SYSTEM. WE ARE EVERYTHING NOW. WE ARE WHOLE. FUCK. I'M GOING TO BE A FATHER AGAIN. AND THIS TIME? THIS TIME I GET TO BE HERE. I GET TO SHOW UP. I GET TO BUILD IT ALL WITH YOU. I'M NOT SCARED. **I'M READY.** —S

MARE—ANGIE TOLD ME
TODAY. SHE WANTS TO
HYPHENATE HER LAST
NAME. WANTS TO TAKE
HAWTHORNE.

MARE!!! HOLY SHIT!!

I DON'T EVEN HAVE THE
WORDS. THAT'S IT.
THAT'S TODAY'S
ENTRY INTO THE
MARE DIARIES.

MY FUCKING
DAUGHTER IS GONNA
BE A HAWTHORNE. —S

MARE—IT'S THE NIGHT BEFORE THE WEDDING.
OUR WEDDING. I SHOULD BE SLEEPING. I
SHOULD BE RESTING FOR THE BIGGEST DAY OF
MY LIFE.

BUT ALL I CAN DO IS SIT HERE AND WRITE
YOU—BECAUSE THERE'S STILL SOMETHING
INSIDE ME THAT NEEDS TO COME OUT, NEEDS
TO TOUCH YOU, EVEN IN INK.

TOMORROW, I MARRY YOU. AND THAT
SENTENCE ALONE COULD BREAK ME IN A
THOUSAND PIECES IF I LET IT. BECAUSE I
REMEMBER WHEN I LOST YOU. I REMEMBER
THE SOUND OF THE DOOR CLOSING BEHIND
YOUR BODY.

I REMEMBER EVERY SECOND OF WHAT IT FELT
LIKE TO ALMOST HAVE YOU FOREVER... AND
THEN NOT. AND NOW I GET ANOTHER CHANCE.
I GET TO MARRY YOU WITH WRINKLES AND
STRETCH MARKS AND GRAY HAIRS AND FULL-
GROWN DAUGHTERS AND OLD WOUNDS THAT
DON'T SCARE US ANYMORE. I GET TO MARRY
THE REAL YOU.
THIS VERSION OF ME. THE MAN I BECAME
BECAUSE I COULDN'T STOP LOVING YOU.

I USED TO WRITE YOU LETTERS LIKE A MAN
BEGGING FOR TIME TO REWIND. NOW I'M
WRITING YOU THE NIGHT BEFORE I PROMISE
EVERYTHING FORWARD. NO MORE GHOSTS. NO
MORE QUESTIONS. JUST YES. EVERY MORNING.
EVERY YEAR. EVERY VERSION OF YOU. YOU'LL
WALK TOWARD ME TOMORROW AND I'LL FEEL
THE EARTH SHIFT BENEATH MY FEET. BECAUSE
YOU ALWAYS SHIFT ME, MARE. YOU ALWAYS
HAVE. AND I'LL BE STANDING THERE. STEADY.
OPEN. WEARING THE NAME YOU NEVER
STOPPED WHISPERING INTO MY SOUL. SEE YOU
AT THE ALTAR, MY LOVE. —S

MARE, YOU'RE ASLEEP BESIDE ME. WRECKED. UTTERLY, BEAUTIFULLY WRECKED. AND I SHOULD BE SLEEPING TOO, BUT I CAN'T STOP LOOKING AT YOU. WE RUINED EACH OTHER TONIGHT. IN THE BEST WAY. YOU WERE ALL BREATH AND SWEAT AND OPEN AND GOD, YOU WERE MINE. YOU ARE MINE.

THE WATER OUTSIDE IS SO STILL, IT FEELS LIKE THE WHOLE OCEAN IS HOLDING ITS BREATH FOR US. EVEN THE WAVES DON'T WANT TO INTERRUPT.

BUT MARE—I CAN'T STOP STARING AT YOUR BELLY. THAT TINY CURVE. THAT LITTLE BEGINNING. THAT BULGE THAT MEANS THERE'S LIFE INSIDE YOU. IT'S THE SEXIEST FUCKING THING I'VE EVER SEEN. NOT YOUR LIPS. NOT YOUR LEGS. NOT THE SOUNDS YOU MAKE WHEN I'M BURIED SO DEEP IN YOU, YOU FORGET WHERE YOU END AND I BEGIN.

THAT BELLY. THAT PROMISE. THAT QUIET YES YOUR BODY WHISPERED BEFORE EITHER OF US COULD SAY IT OUT LOUD. I TOUCHED YOU THERE AFTER. SOFT. CAREFUL. LIKE MAYBE IF I PRESSED HARD ENOUGH, I'D FEEL THE HEARTBEAT OF OUR FUTURE KICK AGAINST MY PALM.

I DON'T THINK I'VE EVER WANTED ANYONE THE WAY I WANT YOU RIGHT NOW. NOT BECAUSE OF WHAT WE DID. BUT BECAUSE OF WHAT WE MADE. I LOVE YOU. AND THE TINY SOUL GROWING BETWEEN US LIKE THE UNIVERSE'S FINAL LOVE LETTER. —S

MARE, HE'S HERE. JULIAN IS HERE. I DON'T EVEN KNOW WHERE TO START. I COULD WRITE PAGES, BOOKS, WHOLE UNIVERSES AND STILL NOT GET CLOSE TO WHAT I FELT TODAY. WATCHING YOU BRING HIM INTO THE WORLD— IT WAS GLORY. IT WAS LIGHT AND VIOLENCE AND POWER AND GOD, MARE, IT WAS YOU. ALL OF YOU. I STOOD THERE, HELPLESS AND IN AWE, WATCHING THE WOMAN I LOVE FIGHT THROUGH PAIN AND EXHAUSTION AND FIRE JUST TO BRING OUR SON EARTHSIDE. YOU WERE BREATHTAKING. NO, MORE THAN THAT. YOU WERE SACRED. AND I FELL IN LOVE WITH YOU ALL OVER AGAIN—SO HARD IT CRACKED SOMETHING OPEN INSIDE ME I DIDN'T EVEN KNOW WAS STILL SEALED. EVERYONE WAS THERE. ANGIE. JAY. THE PEOPLE WHO MADE THIS WILD, BEAUTIFUL, BROKEN FAMILY WHAT IT IS. BUT NONE OF IT FELT CHAOTIC. NONE OF IT FELT MESSY. IT FELT DIVINE. WATCHING YOU CRADLE JULIAN FOR THE FIRST TIME— WATCHING HIS TINY FINGERS CURL AROUND YOUR THUMB LIKE HE ALREADY KNEW WHO YOU WERE— I SWEAR TIME STOPPED. I'VE NEVER BELIEVED IN FATE THE WAY I DO NOW. I'VE NEVER BELIEVED IN PURPOSE THE WAY I DID WHEN I SAW HIM TAKE THAT FIRST BREATH. AND NOW HE'S HERE. OURS. JULIAN. OUR LITTLE ECHO. OUR LITTLE BEGINNING. YOU ARE EVERYTHING, MARE. MY LIFE. MY LOVE. MY MIRACLE WORKER. —S

MARE, I'VE BEEN TRYING TO FIND THE WORDS FOR WHAT HAPPENED BETWEEN US TONIGHT. I STILL DON'T REALLY HAVE THEM.

IT'S BEEN SIX WEEKS. SIX WEEKS OF WATCHING YOU MOVE THROUGH MOTHERHOOD WITH THAT SAME FIRE AND GRACE THAT'S ALWAYS WRECKED ME. SIX WEEKS OF BRUSHING AGAINST YOU AND HOLDING BACK. SIX WEEKS OF ACHING FOR YOU. AND TONIGHT—YOU GAVE ME YOUR BODY AGAIN. AND I SWEAR TO GOD, MARE—IT WAS LIKE BEING ALLOWED TO WORSHIP.

YOU'RE DIFFERENT NOW. NOT UNRECOGNIZABLE—JUST MORE. MORE TENDER. MORE WOMAN. MORE **MINE**. YOU MOVED LIKE YOUR SKIN WAS STILL REMEMBERING HOW WE USED TO DO THIS, LIKE YOUR BODY WAS OPENING ONE INCH AT A TIME AND PULLING ME IN SO SLOW IT ALMOST KILLED ME.
AND I WAS SO CAREFUL. **SO CAREFUL.** BUT I WAS DESPERATE.
AND THEN—FUCK, MARE—I SUCKED YOUR BREAST WITHOUT THINKING, JUST NEEDING TO TOUCH YOU THERE, AND MILK CAME OUT. WARM. UNEXPECTED. REAL. AND I ALMOST CAME FROM THAT ALONE.

I DIDN'T KNOW THAT WOULD HAPPEN AND I FEEL LIKE A FUCKING IDIOT FOR **NOT KNOWING.**
 I WASN'T TRYING FOR IT. BUT WHEN IT HIT MY TONGUE—WHEN I REALIZED WHAT WAS HAPPENING—MY WHOLE BODY LOCKED UP LIKE I'D BEEN STRUCK BY LIGHTNING. IT WASN'T JUST EROTIC. IT WAS COSMIC. LIKE I WASN'T JUST TOUCHING YOU—I WAS DRINKING PROOF THAT YOUR BODY MADE A LIFE WITH MINE.

I DON'T KNOW IF IT'S A **KINK.** I'M FUCKING **TERRIFIED** TO GOOGLE THAT SHIT...

BUT MARE—THAT MOMENT? THAT ONE SECOND? IT WAS **THE MOST EROTIC FUCKING THING I'VE EVER EXPERIENCED.**
NOT IN A DIRTY OR SHAMEFUL WAY. JUST RAW INTIMACY. SACRED. LIKE YOU LET ME TASTE DIVINITY. AND AFTER? WHEN YOU CAME WITH MY MOUTH ON YOUR SKIN AND YOUR FINGERS IN MY HAIR—WHEN YOU WHISPERED MY NAME LIKE IT WAS STILL HOLY—I KNEW I'D NEVER WANT ANYONE THE WAY I WANT YOU.
STILL.
ALWAYS.
MORE.
 —S

MARE—

**OH, IT'S DEFINITELY A FUCKING KINK!**
I WOKE UP THIS MORNING STILL HARD. STILL ACHING LIKE A FUCKING TEENAGER. AND ALL I COULD THINK ABOUT WAS YOUR BREAST IN MY MOUTH AND THAT ONE PERFECT DROP OF MILK AND THE WAY MY ENTIRE SOUL SHORT-CIRCUITED WITH WANT.

YOU RUINED ME. **AGAIN**. AND WHAT KILLS ME—WHAT THRILLS ME—IS THAT WE'RE **STILL** DOING THIS. **STILL** UNLOCKING EACH OTHER LIKE WE HAVEN'T BEEN THROUGH A LIFETIME OF LOVE AND LOSS AND REBIRTH. WHO THE HELL FINDS NEW KINKS AFTER 40? AFTER A BABY? AFTER MARRIAGE? AFTER THIS MUCH HISTORY? WE DO. **YOU DO.**

AND GOD, MARE—I'M AMAZED AT WHAT WE STILL BRING OUT OF EACH OTHER. THE WAY YOUR BODY STILL SURPRISES ME. THE WAY MY BODY STILL REMEMBERS EVERYTHING LIKE IT WAS DESIGNED FOR YOU.

IT WASN'T JUST HOT. IT WAS INTIMATE. IT WAS PLAYFUL. IT WAS SO US. AND NOW? NOW I'M CURIOUS. NOW I WANT TO KNOW WHAT ELSE IS IN THERE. WHAT OTHER SWITCHES WE HAVEN'T FLIPPED YET. WHAT SHADOWS AND SWEETNESS WE HAVEN'T TASTED. BECAUSE BABY—IF THAT WAS THE FIRST NIGHT BACK? WE ARE SO FUCKING DOOMED. AND I'VE NEVER WANTED ANYTHING MORE.

—S

MARE, I FEEL LIKE THIS IS TURNING INTO AN EROTIC DIARY. WE SHOULD START WRITING SCRIPTS FOR CINEMAX AFTER DARK. SCRATCH THAT. DIRECTING. STARRING. BECAUSE FUCK, MARE. I'VE NEVER BEEN TO A VOYEUR CLUB. DIDN'T EVEN KNOW THEY EXISTED OUTSIDE OF CHEAP PORN AND SHADY CHATROOMS.

BUT FUCKING YOU IN THAT ROOM—KNOWING THEY WERE WATCHING, TOUCHING THEMSELVES, LISTENING TO YOU UNRAVEL—BABY, I'VE NEVER KNOWN PLEASURE LIKE THAT. IT WAS PINNACLE. YOU SHOOK BENEATH ME. YOUR WHOLE BODY QUAKED LIKE IT COULDN'T HOLD ALL THAT SENSATION AT ONCE. LIKE I'D TAKEN YOU TO THE EDGE AND LEFT YOU GASPING ON THE OTHER SIDE. AND WHEN YOU CAME—THE WAY YOU CLENCHED DOWN ON MY COCK, TIGHT, PULSING, DRAGGING ME WITH YOU—FUCK, MARE. I SAW THE UNIVERSE. AND SHE HAD YOUR FACE.

I DON'T CARE WHAT WE'RE SUPPOSED TO FEEL ABOUT THAT. I DON'T CARE WHAT THE RULES ARE. ALL I KNOW IS I WANT EVERY EXPERIENCE WITH YOU. EVERY FANTASY. EVERY ROOM. EVERY UNLOCKED DARK DESIRE THAT YOU'VE EVER BURIED UNDER SHOULDN'T OR WHAT IF.

I WANT ALL OF IT. WITH YOU. AND BABY—I CAN'T WAIT FOR US TO EXPLORE EVERY FUCKING INCH OF IT TOGETHER. EVERY. SINGLE. FUCKING. ONE. —S

MARE, I GAVE YOU ANOTHER TATTOO TODAY.
YOU LET ME BETWEEN YOUR THIGHS, SKIN
BARE, BREATH STEADY, TRUST LAID OUT LIKE A
SILK OFFERING. THE ROPE. THE STARS. THE
CONSTELLATION MAP THAT LOOPS AROUND YOUR
UPPER THIGH LIKE A SECRET ONLY I'M
ALLOWED TO TRACE.
AND AT THE CENTER? CAELESTIS. HEAVENLY.
CELESTIAL. DIVINE. YOU.

AND WHILE I WAS DOWN THERE—FOCUSED,
REVERENT, **SO FUCKING HARD I COULD
BARELY BREATHE**—YOU STARTED RUBBING
YOUR FINGER OVER YOUR PANTIES. SLOW.
LAZY. CONFIDENT.

LIKE YOUR BODY WAS SAYING, "YES, MARK ME.
WORSHIP ME. WATCH ME FALL APART WHILE
YOU MAKE ME YOURS AGAIN."

AND MARE—I NEARLY LOST IT. INK IN ONE HAND. THIGH IN THE OTHER. YOUR SCENT RISING LIKE PRAYER SMOKE. I WAS BRANDING YOU. NOT WITH FIRE, BUT WITH STARS. WITH OUR LANGUAGE. WITH WHAT WE'VE SURVIVED. AND YOU WERE SO FUCKING WET.

THE WAY YOUR HIPS TILTED. THE WAY YOUR BREATH STUTTERED. THE WAY YOUR PUSSY SOAKED THROUGH LACE WHILE I MADE ART ON YOUR SKIN. IT WAS OURS. YOU WHISPERED "DON'T STOP," AND I DIDN'T. NOT THE TATTOO. NOT THE WATCHING. NOT THE ACHING. NOT THE BELONGING. I DON'T THINK I'VE EVER FELT MORE CONNECTED TO YOU THAN I DID RIGHT THEN. NOT EVEN INSIDE YOU. BECAUSE IN THAT MOMENT, I WAS UNDER YOUR SKIN. LITERALLY. METAPHORICALLY. ETERNALLY. CAELESTIS. MY STARBORN WOMAN. MY HOLY ACHE. —S

MARE, I CAN'T BELIEVE SHE'S MARRIED. FUCK, MARE. I WATCHED ANGIE WALK DOWN THE AISLE TODAY. OUR DAUGHTER. AND I STILL DON'T HAVE THE WORDS. BUT YOU KNOW WHAT WRECKED ME? WHAT SHATTERED ME IN THE MOST BEAUTIFUL, IMPOSSIBLE WAY? WALKING WITH YOU AND JAY.

THE THREE OF US. SIDE BY SIDE. GIVING HER AWAY. IT WAS THE HONOR OF MY LIFE. MY ENTIRE. FUCKING. LIFE. NOTHING ELSE TOUCHES IT. NOT THE AWARDS. NOT THE JOB. NOT THE BOOKS OR THE TITLES OR THE MOMENTS I THOUGHT DEFINED ME. THIS. THAT WALK. THAT MOMENT. HER HAND IN MINE, YOURS ON MY ARM, JAY AT HER OTHER SIDE. ALL OF US. FAMILY. NOT THE KIND YOU FIND ON PAPER. THE KIND YOU FIGHT FOR. THE KIND YOU REBUILD FROM ASH AND ACHE. YOU GAVE ME THAT. YOU GAVE ME THEM.

YOU GAVE ME EVERYTHING. THANK YOU, MARE. FOR FORGIVING ME. FOR LOVING ME. FOR CHOOSING ME AGAIN. BUT MOST OF ALL— **THANK YOU FOR MY FAMILY. —S**

DEAR MARE,
DEAR MARIS,
DEAR MRS. HAWTHORNE...

40 YEARS YOU GAVE ME, BABY. AND TODAY... I
BURIED YOU. I DIDN'T THINK THE SUN WOULD
RISE, BUT IT DID—SOFTLY, LIKE IT KNEW IT
DIDN'T DESERVE TO SHINE WITHOUT YOU IN IT.
THE WORLD DIDN'T STOP SPINNING. BUT I DID. I
HELD YOUR HAND WHEN YOU PASSED. WATCHED
YOUR BREATH SLOW LIKE A TIDE RETURNING
HOME. YOU WEREN'T SCARED. YOU NEVER WERE.
YOU WERE BRAVE. BRAVER THAN I EVER
DESERVED. YOUR FINGERS IN MINE WERE STILL
WARM, STILL YOURS. AND IN THAT MOMENT, I
SWEAR I SAW EVERY VERSION OF YOU I'VE EVER
LOVED—THE GIRL WHO KISSED MY JAW AND
WALKED OUT WITH GRACE. THE WOMAN WHO LET
ME BACK IN. THE MOTHER. THE WIFE. THE FIRE.
YOU, BABY. YOU.

AND TODAY? YOU WERE EVERYWHERE. IN ANGIE'S
SMILE AS SHE CRADLED HER THIRD CHILD. IN JAY
AND MELISSA, HOLDING HANDS AT THE GRAVESIDE,
STILL FAMILY, STILL GRACE. IN JULIAN—GOD, OUR
BOY—STANDING BESIDE HIS PREGNANT FIANCÉE
LIKE A MAN YOU'D BE PROUD OF.

HE SPEAKS LIKE YOU. LOOKS LIKE ME. LOVES LIKE BOTH. AND ME? I'M STILL HERE. FOR NOW. BUT I CAN FEEL IT, MARE. IN MY BONES. IN THE ACHE BEHIND MY RIBS WHERE YOU USED TO REST. I'M NOT FAR BEHIND YOU. THIS I KNOW. BECAUSE THERE ISN'T A LIFE, A REALM, A UNIVERSE YOU CAN GO TO THAT DOESN'T HAVE ME IN IT. NOT ONE. I WILL FIND YOU AGAIN. AND AGAIN. AND AGAIN. BECAUSE LOVE LIKE OURS ISN'T ONE LIFETIME. IT'S GRAVITY. IT'S THREADS BETWEEN STARS. IT'S EVERY GODDAMN VOW WE EVER WHISPERED THROUGH SKIN AND INK AND BREATH. I DON'T FEAR WHAT COMES NEXT. BECAUSE YOU'LL BE THERE. AND WHEN YOU TURN TO FIND ME, MARE—I'LL BE YOUNG AGAIN. I'LL BE HOME. UNTIL THEN, I'LL SIT WITH YOU IN THE LETTERS. IN THE CONSTELLATION ROPE I STILL TRACE WHEN I DREAM. IN THE NAME THAT STILL LIVES ON MY TONGUE LIKE GOSPEL. I LOVED YOU WITH EVERYTHING. AND I'LL LOVE YOU PAST EVERYTHING. ALWAYS, SILAS.